advance praise fo

NO SUCH THING AS D

"A seductive journey through the melancholy hearts of two men who ought to know better, but who, like the reader, can only acquiesce to the possibility and longing that Donnelly crafts within this tale. I loved it."
—E. Catherine Tobler, author of *A Necessity of Stars*

"At once tender and achingly sharp, like the first breath you take after coming in from the cold."
—Kat Weaver, co-author of *Uncommon Charm*

"*No Such Thing as Duty* is a thrilling alternate history with feverish pacing, whose characters have written themselves into my memory. In this bloodthirsty novella, Donnelly has played her hand, and won."
—Jordan Kurella, author of Nebula-nominated *I Never Liked You Anyway*

"Gritty and decadent and brittle with gallows humor, *No Such Thing as Duty* has everything I want in a story: clever writing, characters sharp enough to cut yourself, and an ending that makes me double-take, then pick up the book and start reading from the beginning. Set aside an afternoon to devour this in one sitting, and thank me later."
—Allison Epstein, author of *Fagin the Thief*

Neon Hemlock Press
www.neonhemlock.com
@neonhemlock

No Such Thing as Duty
Lara Elena Donnelly

Cover Illustration by Juan Gómez Cabello
Interior Design and Layout by dave ring
Edited by dave ring

Print ISBN-13: 978-1-966503-04-0
Ebook ISBN-13: 978-1-966503-05-7

Lara Elena Donnelly

NO SUCH THING AS DUTY

Neon Hemlock Press

NEON HEMLOCK

NO SUCH THING AS DUTY

LARA ELENA DONNELLY

For Jackie, Julia, Rachel, and Rebekah

"FACT IS A POOR STORY-TELLER."

—W. Somerset Maugham,
from the preface to
Ashenden, or: The British Agent

ALL THINGS CONSIDERED, William is glad to be dying in Romania. It is *interesting*, more so than any sanitarium in Scotland. Full of things to look at, people to watch. Even the war is interesting. And it provides him an outlet for that hideous compunction, his sense of duty.

Even now, waiting in the hallway of the consulate to meet the man who will give him his last task on this mortal plane, William mentally composes a letter to his wife: yet another fruit of his questionable chivalry.

He never liked Syrie much at all, even when he wanted her, and knew she had used him with intent toward his money and his name. And he *gave* them to her, more fool him. More fool him for ever looking at her twice. Because he will be embarrassed about the situation until the end of his life (any day now), the letter is cruel: *I know it will suit you well if I die so far from home,* it says. He will never send this letter, because he would not want his daughter Liza to see it when she's grown. What child would want to understand that it had been so used? That its good name was given only grudgingly?

At least he can rest assured that Liza will be taken care of in his will. But he might have liked to know her, when she was old enough to really know. When he might resent her less for her mother's use of her to trap him in this farcical marriage.

He wonders briefly about Gerald, who he has not heard from since April, when—just after their return from Tahiti, just before William's music hall joke of a wedding—he enlisted and left for training. William sometimes wonders if he made it, or if his ship was torpedoed and sank. Maybe he's found someone else to keep him company. He never lacked for opportunities, and rarely left one unexploited, even under William's nose. The army is surely providing endless options. William can't summon up any jealousy. Gerald is young and healthy. If he's still alive, he ought to be enjoying it. Enjoying life always looked good on him.

A door opens into the corridor where William is waiting for his appointment.

"Mr. Maugham," says the secretary. "Mr. Max will see you now."

The office is grand but messy: boxes stacked against every wall, drifts of folders and paper, more boxes on chairs pulled in from other rooms. The desk does not match the woodwork or the architecture. A hasty set up in a building not meant to serve the purpose. An ugly green desk lamp sits unlit on its corner, made superfluous by the blue white light pouring in through the French windows. Jassy is covered in dirty snow, more snow falling.

The windows also let in the cold. Max has a scarf around his neck—Oriel—and his hands are red and chapped.

"Mr. Maugham," he says, and indicates the chair across from him. "Or should I say Mr. Somerville?"

William moves the stack of maps and telegrams discreetly to the floor. Somerville is just for customs, a name for strangers, but he doesn't correct Max. He doesn't want an answer, anyway.

William is supposed to be meeting with Captain Thomas Laycock, who is leading the Bureau in Romania. But Laycock is busy, or elsewhere, or can't be bothered, so he's been shuffled off to this fellow. Gilbert Max is not really the Second Assistant to the Military Attaché. Or, he *is,* but the mission doesn't need him, so he has plenty of time for other pursuits. William imagines Romania's armistice with the Central Powers has provided pursuits aplenty.

"This is a strange time for an English novelist to be in Jassy," says Max. "What are you supposed to tell people?"

This question does want an answer. William steels himself, trying to picture the sentence stretching out before him like a long, unbroken road.

"I'm working on a series of articles for th…the…" God damn it, he can *feel* the word stuck behind his teeth. He's exhausted already from the travel, from his illness. The effort to get from one end of a statement to another feels Herculean.

"Brandy?" Max gets up, already headed for the sideboard, uncomfortable or impatient or uncaring, or any number of other things people always feel and sometimes try to hide when William has a go at a fence and his words balk.

"*Times,*" he says, and bites down hard once he gets the word out. Bites down on his own anger, like he can behead it. "Please."

The brandy makes him cough, and tuberculosis makes him keep on coughing until he is dizzy. Bright black spots pepper the edges of his peripheral vision.

Max looks politely into the middle distance while William gasps into his handkerchief. When he's done, the conversation continues as if it had never been interrupted. Everyone here knows the score. Nobody—except Syrie, in willful ignorance—expects him to come home.

"May I be frank?" asks Max.

He nods again.

"We've had a very good account of the work you did in Petrograd, despite the outcome. Macdonagh's people said if you'd got there six months earlier you might have made a difference for the Eastern front. Laycock liked your Czechoslovak strategy; pity it won't play out."

William sits quiet, waiting for the rest.

Max girds himself, then addresses his towering inbox. "Masaryk's been in Jassy and it seems he doesn't want anything to do with the Romanians. He thinks it's a doomed country, and I think he's right, whatever Laycock says. Without the Czechoslovaks, there's no chance of linking up with the Cossacks in the Don. Kaledin's people are a mess, anyway; all talk. Romania's armistice will end in a treaty with Germany. It's just a matter of time, and not much of it."

"But," William says, before he can stop himself. And now he's committed. "Sir. In London…they seemed quite certain—"

"As I'm sure you're aware, having just made the journey, London is worlds away from the situation here."

In the cold and the flattening snow light, William feels every mile of the trip. His back still aches from days and nights on the train. He is tired and his chest is sore. Fever makes his clothes itch against his skin. He wants to lie down and sleep right here, on top of Max's telegrams.

"I won't t…turn around and go back," he said. "Can't you give me something?"

"Get some rest, for now," says Max. "We've arranged a flat. If anything comes up, we'll be in touch."

Well there it is. He's come all this way and left Liza without a father, telling himself there was a greater purpose he could fulfill. A lie. There is no great cause, no doing his bit, no satisfaction for his self-destructive sense of duty. All he really wanted was to get away from his failures.

But, he thinks, as he shuffles out the door and into the snowy street, how much longer would Liza have had him? The sanitarium was no sure thing. He could have died as easily in Britain as Romania. A comforting thought.

His bitter laugh makes him breathe the cold air, and he coughs into his muffler. The wool grows wet, but it's black and won't show a stain.

HIS FLAT IS small, with a bright sitting room overlooking a courtyard and a dark bedroom overlooking an air shaft. There is a gas ring, but no food to speak of in the larder. He gets into bed fully clothed and falls asleep.

It's dark when he wakes up, and the snow has stopped. His fever is down and he's ravenous. They've delivered his luggage to the flat, and he puts on dry socks and boots before venturing into the frozen streets.

He finds a café with steamy windows and orders in French. Soon he has a small hot cup of bitter coffee and a boiled cheese donut. He sits by the windows, though the cold rolls off the glass, because he likes the softening effect of the condensation, like he is enveloped in fog.

He has been surprised, so far, to learn that cities at the fringes of war are much like cities that are not. In Petrograd you could still get a cup of scalding tea, see a Chaplin picture, even when they started shooting people in the streets. In the corner here, someone plays a piano. It has a few dead keys, and is generally in poor tune, but the noise is cheerful. He sits deep in his chair and pulls a notebook from the pocket of his jacket, a pen tucked inside.

He wishes briefly for Gerald, who would already be fast friends with the raucous group of young men in the café, their table cluttered with coffee cups and shot glasses.

Gerald who is younger, better-looking, and unafraid. Gerald who, if his boat hasn't been sunk, is no doubt facedown in a ditch, drunk or dead. The war was supposed to sober him up, but what William has seen of the war so far seems likely to drive even teetotalers to drink. Nothing he saw in Lambeth, not the breach births or the advanced syphilis or the workers' hands crushed in heavy machinery…none of it prepared him for the kinds of things he treated at the front. Men have always killed each other, but never quite like this.

«You are a writer?»

He looks up from his notebook, which he has laid out on the table. The page is half-filled with notes from the final leg of his train journey: a description of the passing land, blanketed with snow. The elderly conductor. A snatch of conversation between two weary officers, speaking French: what would they eat when they got home? Some of the words he had not recognized. These are written out phonetically, so he can ask someone what they mean.

Someone, perhaps, like this young man.

He nods, because he rarely trusts himself to speak to strangers. It cements a certain first impression. It's what he likes—liked—Gerald for. With Gerald around, he never had to do much talking.

«What do you write?» the young man asks. His French is serviceable. He has heavy good looks, a body that will run to fat as he gets older. His army cap and army coat are worn over a plain suit of worsted. The armistice has left the country in a state of similar arrested transition. Max told him to watch out for Russian deserters loitering in Jassy, and the fights they start; told him there are women who aren't even sure they're widows, wondering when—or if—their husbands will come home.

William wants to say that he writes *plays* but the word looms, impossible even in French, and so he jinks to the side and says «Dramas. And novels.»

«You are English?»

He nods again, amused. Born in Paris, French was his first tongue and he does not speak it the way an Englishman does. Something more indelible must have given him away.

The young man takes his nod as some kind of invitation, or at least acquiescence, and sits in the empty chair at William's table. «Please do not hold the armistice against me,» he says. «I am called Mihai. And you?»

«William,» he says.

«Have I seen your plays?» asks Mihai.

William shakes his head. He doesn't think they've done *Jack Straw* in Bucharest.

«Are they any good?»

William shrugs, and smiles.

Mihai looks at him with frank speculation, playfulness sharpening into a familiar kind of assessment. «You don't talk much, do you?» He doesn't sound like he minds.

William's grip on his pen tightens, and he taps it with finality on the page. «I…prefer to write.» He makes the last consonant crisp as he can.

Mihai's expression closes, and he stands. «I respect a man's preference,» he says, and goes back to his friends.

William did not come to Romania for fun. He did not come to mine the rich veins of varied human experience. He came to do a job for King and country. And while King and country seem temporarily at a loss for what is to be done with him, William has that stubborn streak of honor he cannot seem to scour out.

He finishes his cheese donut and his coffee. He has lost his appetite for anything more, except the work he came to do. If they can find any to give him.

A WEEK GOES BY, much the same. He writes the first few scenes of a story, moves them around and then moves them back. Drinks coffee, eats pastries, buys coal; the war has made everything expensive. He writes letters he won't be able to send until the next diplomatic bag goes out. Coughs and coughs and catches his breath, coughs again.

Before he was a celebrated playwright, a novelist, a spy, William was a physician at St. Thomas's in Lambeth. He did the years of training, cut up cadavers, rushed through the worst streets in London at the worst possible hours to deliver sickly babies starving families didn't want. He knew he had tuberculosis before his diagnosis, but was very good at pretending he didn't. Now he is very good at pretending it isn't getting worse.

He should be lying down and resting, keeping his blood pressure low. In a sanitarium they'd have him staring peaceably into the middle distance and taking shallow breaths. Instead, he walks the streets when the weather cooperates. Jassy is a beautiful city even in winter, even when one is half-delirious with fever, even though its streets and buildings have been stripped and repurposed for war and the sudden influx of an exiled government and all its trappings.

Speaking of: he's summoned back to Max's office by courier, a weedy young man swallowed by his uniform, face red with cold under the brim of his hat. William allows himself to be bundled into the back of a car and driven to the embassy. He nods off on the way, bones aching and clothes rough on his prickling skin, and dreams briefly of sinking into the snow.

The jerk of the brakes abruptly wakes him. He is soaked in sweat and shivering.

Max blanches when he comes into the office, but covers it quickly. "All right?" he asks. "Sit down before you fall down. Coffee?"

William nods, catching his breath. Max pours from a

silver pot. The coffee is tepid. It is not much warmer in Max's office than it was in the car. Max himself looks like he has not slept since William left him last.

"You're a lucky man, Mr. Maugham," he says. "I've got something for you after all." He slides a folder across the desk and William flips it open. A photo is clipped to the verso side of the cover: a handsome man, old for his thirties but young for his fifties, true age elided by a full beard and the flattering uniformity of white tie. There is a row of medals pinned to his breast.

"Walter Roşu," Max tells him, just as William reads the name himself: *Roşu, Walter. Place of Birth: Vienna. Date of Birth: Unknown. Profession: Unknown.* William skims the notes—*independent income, unmarried, possibly homosexual*—while Max goes on. "And before you ask, no, we don't know much more than that."

Max grimaces at the folder. "We're told he can get his hands on anything anybody needs. Get into and out of any place anybody needs him to go. Like a bloody rat, they say: squeezing though the cracks. Nobody knows how he does it, but they do know he's rich, and cagey, and he never gets caught."

"A s—" He feels it waver, on the verge of failing. The pause before he speaks gives the word that follows undue significance. "Smuggler."

Max raises his eyebrows. "I don't care if he is."

This seems worth knowing, and so he steels himself to ask: "And...what do you need smuggled?"

"We're exfiltrating agents," Max tells him. "As many as we can, as fast as we can, before Romania signs a treaty and the Germans get free rein over their papers and our people. And we've been doing an all right job of it so far."

"But."

"We had an agent in Bucharest," says Max. "A woman. We hadn't heard from her in months—victim of the occupation, we thought. But she's raised a signal.

Wants out, and what's more, she says she has valuable intelligence for us. Can't be sent by courier, can't be wired. Face to face only, she says. Anything else is too risky." Max scowls. "Bloody female agents. Hysterics and drama over something she could probably send en clair from the local telegraph office. Still, some jobs you just can't send a man, can you?"

William fights the corners of his mouth, which wants to smile.

"Anyway," Max goes on. "Obviously Bucharest is impossible for an Englishman. But local gossip says this Roşu's been in and out at least twice since the Huns took over. Third time's a charm, and if he can't get her out maybe he knows someone who can."

"Sir," says William, and marshals his wits. "I'm grateful for the chance, but surely there are people more qualified? I don't know the city. I d…don't have any connections."

Max sighs, beleaguered. "This isn't some *bone* I'm throwing you, Maugham. I didn't grub up some work to make you feel useful. But I'll be honest: I'm not sure of the value of the intelligence, I can't risk my good agents in enemy territory, and I haven't got anybody to spare to chase around some queer Romanian aristocrat who might be all smoke and mirrors."

"Aristocrat?" asks William, leaving the other descriptor on the table between them. Unlike Max, he won't bely himself with protestations. The mission is a sop. A throwaway. So much for a duty greater than death.

But it was never the duty he was dying for, was it? No matter what he told himself. Apologies, Liza. When you're older maybe you'll understand. Especially if you get older living under the same roof as Syrie.

"His family has some land in the mountains, titles older than the empire. Anyway, you don't *need* connections, do you? You're a famous bloody writer, everyone knows who you are. If you want introductions, have your editor send some letters. Hell, have him send telegrams and save his receipts. We'll reimburse."

"To whom?"

Some tension goes out of Max's shoulders, having foisted this half-job onto somebody else's plate. There's a stack of papers in his inbox higher than the lid of his coffee pot. "I'll make a list."

This dismissal is plain. William gathers his coat around him—he never took it off when he arrived, nor his scarf nor gloves. Before he puts his hat back on, he asks, "Max, the agent. Who is she?"

Max grimaces. "I'm not going to give you the cart if you haven't got a horse, Maugham. Get me Roşu first."

William wishes now that he had taken Mihai home. Wishes he had misbehaved a little more, if this is the sacred duty accorded him by his government: find a man we don't think much of and ask him to retrieve a woman we might have preferred dead.

Gerald would have taken Mihai up on his offer, in front of William's face, too. And if there had only been one bedroom in their rented flat, then he'd have done a number of other things in front of William's face as well.

Suddenly, fiercely, William misses the South Pacific. He misses the heat. The indolence. The fecundity and rot and Gerald sweating next to him, naked under the useless mosquito netting. He knew where he stood with Gerald, who wanted his money and his name, much like Syrie, but was happy to take them on William's terms.

He misses, too, the incredible, bald-faced lie of colonial society. In those isolated patches of the empire, convention was of such sustaining importance it didn't really matter what a person *did*. Appearances needn't even be kept up as long as you arrived on time for tea. Under the southern cross there was no such thing as duty. There was only the pantomime thereof: a tawdry spectacle as likely to make you laugh as cry. He misses watching it all unfold, secretly storing away facts and anecdotes and assessing them later for their potential.

War work is a similar analysis of the human condition, but on a grander scale: not a drawing room comedy or family drama, but an opera, an epic. The follies of nations, the character of their leaders. One man's opinion moving multitudes, and how that opinion and therefore the multitudes might be swayed in a favorable direction.

It does all, he supposes, still come down to people. Maybe that's why he's been good at it so far.

Speaking of people:

One of the names on his list is Maria Popescu, heiress and well-known patron of the arts. Widowed not even a year ago. Max's note says she and Roşu were close before her husband's death; he often attended her dinner parties. She should still be in mourning but this war has upended everything, even the stuffy rituals of grief. She goes out. She is seen in town. She and Roşu are invited to the same social engagements, inasmuch as society struggles on. William wonders why Max doesn't use her right out, until he arrives in her drawing room and finds, among the other guests, two German officers and a Turkish diplomat drinking coffee while Maria's daughter plays Mozart's eleventh sonata. He does his best not to freeze on the threshold.

«M. Maugham!» Mme. Popescu sweeps across the thick Persian rug, footfalls muffled. Her hands are long-fingered and fine, posed in a careful clasp against her breast. Black suits her. «It is such an incredible honor. Please, come sit. Will you have coffee?»

«Yes,» he says, «Thank you.» With a practiced hostess's grace, she seats him across the room from the enemy.

Of course it is not treasonous for her to host these

men—Romania is not at war with the Central Powers anymore. But it still feels strange to catch those high gray collars from the corner of his eye, to hear French consonants attacked with German precision.

He distracts himself with the other guests. It is unlikely Roşu will be here—that would be too convenient. But he likes to look at people, generally. Likes to watch their little dramas, note their tics and foibles.

There is a girl, freshly out, nervous fingers on the naked skin of her neck. Poor thing, what husbands are there to find these days? She is paying little attention to the music but much attention to the gentlemen in the room, though none of them can possibly be suitable. Her mother watches her with as much focus, also ignoring the Mozart. An elderly artistic type has backed two other women against the window and is gesticulating intensely as he describes something neither of them has much interest in. As William watches, they edge away toward the sideboard and make a great show of examining some Sèvres figurines. Both wear half mourning: pale purple and pearly silver, like the downy breasts of doves.

Still his eyes wander back to the sharp gray tunics. He can't stop them following the Turkish functionary around the room.

«They make you nervous,» says Mme. Popescu, returning from a round of small talk.

He gives her a noncommittal smile.

«This is a salon,» she says. «Not a battlefield. Not even a bargaining table. Romania is not at war.»

He shakes his head. «Apologies, I am being rude.»

She smiles, dark eyes soft. «Hardly. If anything, you are being remarkably civil.»

Women often think he is civil. Attentive. Polite. Mostly because he doesn't talk much. But he has to keep up his end of the conversation now, because he isn't here to make up numbers at a table. He has a job to do.

«Isn't it…awkward?» he asks, only faltering a little.

«For whom?» she asks. «Do I not have an Englishman here as well? A French painter?» Here she inclines her head toward the artistic type. «Even a few Americans. If it's awkward, we are all sharing the burden. But I prefer to imagine we are briefly setting awkwardness aside to enjoy a little music.» Then she sighs, suddenly melancholy. «The armistice won't last, I think. Best to make use of it.»

«You don't think so?» It's the same thing Max had said, or nearly. «Will it fall out for us or them?»

She raises an eloquent eyebrow: a dark slash emphasizing her expression like a diacritic. «You will notice,» she says, «that I have two German officers, and only one English novelist.» Here she pauses, scrutinizing him with an intensity unwarranted by the hostess of an artistic afternoon. «What *are* you doing in Jassy, M. Maugham? It is an odd time and an odd place for an Englishman.»

This one is easy, and much rehearsed: the bread and butter of his time spent in Geneva, the very reason the Bureau ever thought he could be useful. «Well, Madame,» says William. «Odd perhaps for an Englishman. But for a writer?»

Her laughter is coquettish, with a sharp undertone like the mineral base of a crisp white wine. She sparkles like one too. «You came all the way to Jassy to write a little book about us? In the middle of a war?»

«I'm on assignment from the *Times*,» he says, having said it enough now it comes out smooth.

She tuts, tongue against her teeth. «A waste of your talents, I think.»

«War asks sacrifices of us all.» He lays his hand on her arm: consolation, and to keep her from flitting away. «And I'm afraid I must ask a small one of you, now.»

☦

«I JUST CAN'T IMAGINE what you'd want with Walter.»

That's what she'd said, but William doesn't believe her. She seems like the kind of person with a very active imagination.

Still, she sends a note to Roşu for him—«He is a great man of letters, M. Roşu—» and soon they have set a date to meet.

William wonders what Mme. Popescu's letter said. He is not in the habit of false modesty, and can understand that anyone might want to meet W. Somerset Maugham, celebrated author and playwright. He is not quite sure how Mme. Popescu might have framed his desire to meet with Walter Roşu, suspected smuggler.

What had he told her? He was so tired by the end of the night he could hardly keep track of what he was saying. A miracle he could still string together a sentence. A miracle he left standing on his own feet. His stammer has always made socializing exhausting. His illness makes *everything* exhausting.

Perhaps he said that he had heard a great deal about M. Roşu from a friend. His family was quite established in the area, correct? That he would like to speak to him about how things have changed since the war began. Something like that.

Did she believe it? She pretended to, at least. And now William is being ushered into the foyer of an impressive house on the outskirts of the city: a white stucco building with dozens of red tiled roofs, somewhere between a monastery and a palace. It is early evening, already dark, and even in the marble splendor of the entryway his breath makes mist in front of his face.

The majordomo returns after a moment, takes his coat, leads him down a series of narrow passages with high ceilings lost to shadow, until they reach a door shut against the chill. Firelight licks the parquet from underneath the door.

«M. Maugham,» says the majordomo, and bows him into the room.

It is a library, with a table set for two in front of the fireplace. One chair is empty. The other is filled with Walter Roşu.

He is a tall man, well-formed, with thick, dark hair a little long for London fashion. He wears a luxurious mustache and a neatly trimmed beard: civilized, but unabashedly of the East. His lower lip is full and ripe under the facial hair. Over a sharp modern dinner jacket, he wears an open smoking jacket of thick brocade.

«M. Maugham,» he says, and does not rise or offer his hand to shake. Somehow the lapse does not feel rude, but right. William sweeps his tails out of the way to sit, and finds himself looking up at a slight angle. He wonders if this is the difference in their heights, or if his chair is lower.

Max told him Walter was from an old family, boyars or noblemen or something. If Max had known, William would have remembered. But Max didn't *want* to know, not in the way that William's writer's brain craves details and specifics. It had been diplomat's homework for him, and he had other, more important exams to sit just now.

Boyars, he imagines, don't shake hands.

«M. Roşu,» he says, pronouncing it correctly. He had paid close attention to Mme. Popescu's pronunciation, which differed significantly from Max's. Max had not made the effort. Because he isn't really a diplomat, is he? He's a spy.

But so is William, and he still went to the trouble.

"We can speak English, if you prefer," says Roşu.

«Thank you,» says William. «But I'm q…quite comfortable in French.» As a child on the Champs-Élysées, he could speak it without a stammer. Then his mother died, and his father, and he was sent to England and his life and language changed so suddenly it seemed to take the words straight out of his mouth. Unfortunately he's brought the bad habit from his second language back into his first.

—Russian too, and German, I hear, says Roşu, in the first language. He pours brandy for them both and finishes in the second. „You must keep very busy."

«I'm an author,» says William, wondering where Roşu learned about his multilingual fluency. «I…like words.» Then, ruefully admitting his stammer: «Though sometimes they don't like me.»

«Well,» says Roşu, «They must yearn to take their vengeance on such a merciless taskmaster. How many books and plays by now? Twenty-odd, I think. An impressive output for a man so young.»

William laughs, because they must be close to the same age, and that age is middling; Roşu has five years on him at most, for all his modern attitude toward evening wear. Roşu's answering smile, though, is tinged with irony. Like he is laughing at a different joke.

«Do you read many English novels?» William asks.

«I am an avid reader in many languages» says Roşu, «Though I will admit to a preference for the Russians, especially those who take a very long view. A refreshing perspective, I think. I enjoy an epic.»

Through the soup, they discuss Russian literature, and then, with the fish, the ancient epics of India, China, and Japan. They are onto Norse mythology by the main course—pork cooked a little rare for William's taste, and a crime in a country where meat has become illegal, on a continent where war-time deprivation is the norm—and then opera with the salad and theatre by coffee and dessert. Roşu has startling recall for verse and prose and song, quoting back lyrical passages from Beowulf and singing a scrap of "Abendlich strahlt der Sonne Auge" in a wry, self-deprecating baritone.

Against his better judgment, William is charmed. He knows this is dangerous, when dealing with an asset. First, because they cannot be trusted. Second, because they can be killed, and sometimes must be. There is now some dubious comfort in the idea that Max's intelligence about Roşu might be wrong, or that the mission might be unimportant.

Then Roşu folds his napkin and drops it onto the table and says, «What a pleasant change. Most people do not call on me to spend an evening discussing culture.»

«To their very great loss.»

«Mine, I'm afraid.» He seems disinclined to give any more of an entrée, putting William at a disadvantage.

«Why do people c…c…call on you?» asks William. And though he struggles mightily in the middle of the sentence Walter merely waits, expression bland and pleasant, until he gets it out. Like he has all the time in the world.

«For my discretion, usually.» But he softens it with a laugh. «I enjoyed myself, M. Maugham. I hope you will call again.»

«I would like that very much,» he says.

AND SO THE courtship begins. And it *is* a courtship with assets, it always is. This time the metaphor is simply… more exact.

They dine at Walter's weekly. It is Walter now, not Roşu, at his request, and he calls William Willie—a diminutive he has always preferred over his Christian name.

Walter stands too close. He lets his hand linger on William's forearm after making a point. And William, mostly, lets him. What harm can it do, behind closed doors? But Walter persists even on the street, in restaurants, at the theatre. It's clear what he wants, and he is handsome, but he's dangerously indiscreet. *Possibly homosexual* indeed. Does he think his wealth protects him? His family?

Whatever it is, it won't extend to William, who resents being put in the position. Usually. But there are moments—Walter grasping William's chin, tipping his face to examine the barber's work; Walter wiping a trace of sour cream from the corner of William's mouth, sucking his fingertip clean—when desire weakens William's resolve and he feels somehow like crying. Sexual desire, yes, but also desire for something he can't quite name. Even Gerald, who flirted like a whore, knew when to stiffen his spine and clench his jaw and give a certain kind of impression. Walter's ease, his assurance, is impossibly seductive. William wants. He *wants*. But he will not let himself have.

He writes reports, also weekly, and encodes them for the embassy to send along. Max has the cipher, this time, unlike Buchanan in Petrograd, and so he can read what William writes. Does he? Have any of William's assiduously encoded messages made it across the channel? Not that they'd do much good. What is he up to, after all? The theatre, with Walter. Buying art, with Walter. An architectural tour of Jassy's oldest synagogue, though Walter runs very late and arrives halfway through, after the sun has gone down and the light no longer catches the edges of the stones, the gilding.

They go out after, to a plush café that Walter tells him once served coffee in the Viennese style, when cream was easier to come by. The shell-shaped windows, the wrought iron curves, wrap around banquettes of red velvet and tables of satiny dark wood. William feels like he is in Paris, twenty years ago. He feels younger, and not as tired as he should.

Tuberculosis can make one feel this way. Enervated, flushed, even sexually ravenous. It is the shock of feeling well in between downturns, or maybe the heat of the fever heightening every other sensation. The surreal saturation of the world when one's brain is simmering at thirty eight degrees.

But maybe it's just the architecture, the good weather, the thrill of Walter's conversation. That's possible.

«Coffee,» Walter tells the waiter. «And…» here he looks at William, intently, and finishes: «Just coffee, I think.»

«Mind reader,» says William, struggling only a little to get the words over the starting line. It is easier to talk with Walter, who never hurries him. Never tries, like some people do, to finish his sentences for him. As if they are running out of time, not him.

«You don't look hungry,» says Walter. «Was I wrong?»

In their short acquaintance, he never has been. If anyone could finish William's sentences the way he wants to, maybe it's Walter.

There is a rowdy table not too far away: men, mostly, older and not as drunk as the soldiers on his first night in Jassy had been. Still, it reminds him of Mihai, and missed chances. And of something else.

«Walter,» he says, and takes his notebook from his breast pocket. Walter watches with interest as he flips through, looking for the thing his memory has snagged on. He finds it earlier than he expected, surprised he has filled so many pages.

«What do these words mean?» he asks, tapping the soldiers' transcribed conversation. «Food, I know, but what kind?»

Walter tilts his head to read. He splays his fingers across the paper, their tips pressed against its grain like he can squeeze more meaning from the words. The pressure makes white crescents at the tips of his manicured nails.

«He is saying ciorbă,» says Walter, and spells it. William writes. «It is a soup. This kind specifically is made with…well, you would call it spinach, but it is not, quite.»

«And this?»

Walter laughs, like it is a joke meant just for him.

«Blood sausage. He'll have to wait until next Christmas, unless his mother is very accommodating.» He flattens his hand against the paper and sweeps it across, smoothing the page so flat the ghost of the next can be seen through it. «It is fascinating to see the world like this. The way you see it. Hear it.» With his middle finger, he raises the lower corner of the page. «May I?»

He would not have let Syrie do it, not in a thousand years. He had only shown Gerald select pages: transcriptions of stories he had brought back from card games, snatches of invented dialogue for the characters they met at the captain's table. A gauge of his own humor and accuracy.

But in Walter's posture and tone there is a balance of deference, interest, and entitlement that strikes a hidden bullseye in William's writer's heart. And in some other heart as well. He could say no; but Walter *wants* to see. And what's more, Walter believes he wants to show him.

William removes his own hand from the notebook and gestures for Walter to take it. Their coffees arrive. Walter laughs at something he has read, and turns a page.

«Will you write a book about your time here?» he asks. «Or maybe a play?»

Mme. Popescu had asked the same question. People are always so eager to see themselves immortalized. «Maybe. I never know, when I write things down.»

«Why do you write them, then?»

William shrugs. «I find people very interesting.»

Walter goes through the rest of the journal thoughtfully, lingering over passages, unhurried. William resists the urge to lean forward, to try to see which parts he's reading closely. When Walter finally does close the journal, he puts a heavy hand on the back cover and strokes his thumb across the leather. It makes a soft sound: the whisper of skin on skin.

«You observe them from the outside,» he says. «As if you are not one of them.»

Is that not the usual position of a writer? A mental distance one takes, like a hunter in a blind? And yet, with Walter he wants to be honest. He does not step away to gain his perspective; he is a queer orphan born on the wrong side of the Channel, who cannot even speak to others without immense effort. Since an early age, he has been on the outside, looking in. «I often feel I'm not.»

Walter nods, as if he knows. And he would, wouldn't he? With a family so old, a position so elevated. He must be intimate with the isolation of a great height.

«I do sometimes find it lonely,» William says, guessing.

A deep furrow appears between Walter's brows, and William intuits from that furrow the fear that ancient peasants must have felt at the displeasure of his ancestors.

«But often—» placating but still honest, eager to make the furrow disappear without growing obsequious—«it is a very great relief. People seem to expect so much…» And here, he realizes, is the thing that ties him to the rest of humanity, that always draws him back despite his artist's objectivity. This horrible sense of obligation he wishes he could shed. «Sometimes it costs less, to be alone.»

The furrow has gone from Walter's brow. He gives the journal back. «Well put.»

WHEN THEY FINISH their coffee, it is late and William is swaying in his seat. Walter offers to walk him home.

The weather has warmed in the last week, slightly, but the nights are still bitter. Walter wraps a muffler over his mouth. William's breath condenses in the air, uneven clouds rising in the soft yellow flicker of the lamps. The cold, damp air makes his chest ache in a familiar way. His breath comes more raggedly. And then, inevitably, he begins to cough.

It is the kind of cough he does not like to have in front of other people: the kind that goes on and on and *hurts*, good Christ, until he feels like he could gag. He presses his handkerchief against his lips so hard his teeth cut into them. When he finally draws breath again, and lowers the linen, it is stippled with red. He swallows, tests the inside of his mouth with his tongue to taste for blood, to wipe it away.

When he looks up at last, Walter is staring, frozen: his shoulders do not even move to breathe. The small flames of the lamps are reflected like pinpoints in his eyes, which are otherwise lightless black.

«You are ill,» he says at last, as though he is remembering how to speak.

William nods, still catching his breath. He puts a hand out, groping for a lamp post or a pillar box or anything to lean against. He finds Walter's shoulder. The other man must have moved—he had not been reaching in that direction.

«Consumption,» says Walter, like it is a rare and precious treasure. He puts a hand over William's hand. «It is very advanced.»

If not for his showy polyglot demonstration the night that they first met, William would have shrugged off the statement as a slight mistranslation; something that should have been a question. But it does not have the rising tone of a question, by which interrogation can be assumed even across languages. Walter speaks as if he has counted William's pulse, listened to the breath laboring in his chest. Speaks as if he knows. It doesn't feel like there's much point in denying things.

«Yes,» says William. «I won't be going back to England. Not out of a b…box, anyway.»

There is a stark pause, and then Walter smiles—slightly forced—and says «Better than steerage.»

William obliges him by laughing—a brief, pained huff—

and then takes his hand from Walter's shoulder at last. Walter's hand lingers at the decorative epaulet of his coat, as if he regrets the loss.

They walk on silently until they reach William's building. Walter looks around the empty nighttime street, eyes narrow. Taking in the shabby splendor, decades out of date. The darkened windows and dirty banks of snow.

«I know,» says William, hoarse. «Not exactly…B… Belgravia, is it?» And this time it is the struggle against his stammer that sets him off. The last two words crumble into another fit of coughing, his frantic ragged inhales catching on the raw edges left by his earlier fit.

There's blood in his mouth, on the back of his teeth, his tongue. He is searching for his handkerchief, which seems to have fallen from his pocket. Black spots like snowflakes swirl at the edges of his vision. He staggers, because he has lost any sense of the ground under his feet.

Walter catches his elbow before he falls, but his feet tangle and he can't get his legs underneath him. He is going to collapse against Walter's chest, but then—

Walter has him up, has him pressed into the vestibule of his own front door, back against the cold stones of the wall, and—and, he's *kissing* him. Here, in the street. The soft scrape of beard against his chin, and Walter's mouth open against his. Sucking his lower lip, tongue sliding beneath his upper, against the front of his teeth. Searching, hungry, deepening the kiss so that William cannot catch his traitorous breath.

The kiss tastes salty, ferric. The sticky slip of blood is between their lips, turning tacky where it dries.

A moment later, blinking, he is standing straight with two strong hands around his arms, staring at three red dots of different sizes freckling Walter's shirt front. He makes himself look up.

Walter's beard is glistening around his mouth and his full lower lip is filmed with William's blood. When he smiles it has soaked in between his teeth, giving each one a crisp and grisly definition.

«I—» He shakes his dizzy head. «Walter. Out here? Anyone could have…could have…!» *Seen.* The dark windows that line the street stare down like rows and rows of eyes. The lamp in the vestibule makes a perfect circle on the pavement like a spotlight.

Walter runs his hands down the lapels of William's coat, lets his right palm rest over William's heart, so they can both see his knuckles jump with every desperate beat. *I want, I want, I want.*

«Well then,» says Walter. «You had better invite me in.»

In the hairpin turns of the stairwell, William's own breath echoes back at him: hard, fast, maybe because it is difficult to climb the stairs, maybe because Walter is climbing the stairs just behind him. Their footsteps creak, louder than William remembers from just this morning. Every sound is louder, every sense heightened, and Walter a curious blank behind him: absolutely silent.

His keys rattle in the lock. Walter puts a firm hand between his shoulder blades. The door swings open and shows a sharply cut rectangle of white light across the floor. The moon is pouring through the sitting room window, silvering the edges of all the furniture and turning the pale upholstery ghostly white.

Walter, too, is ghostly white, his cheekbones and brow eerie between the darkness of his beard and swept-back hair. He shuts the door behind him and William hears the resonant impact of the bolt sliding home.

They stand in the moonlight, William's back not so far from the wall, Walter's mouth not so far from his own.

«I'm married,» says William, disclosing it like a shameful illness or deformity. Like he is offering Walter a chance to change his mind, and almost hoping that he might. He is scared, suddenly, because he wants this so badly. It is an intensity of feeling he has not allowed himself since his diagnosis. Since he parted ways with Gerald. Since he bowed to the inevitable, and went before the judge with Syrie. Desiring anything seemed pointless and painful, when death was so near and every other desire had ended in disaster.

Walter's eyes are black as pitch, and looking into them William has a sense they might catch fire just as easily. William lifts one hand, trembling, unsure what he is reaching out to touch—

And then Walter is on him, a sudden surge of muscle and hunger, and they are wrestling with each other's coats and scarves and heavy winter woolens.

He does not make love like Gerald, playful and boyish, nor with the tender abandon of William's long-lamented Sue, the woman he should have married and missed getting by the breadth of a hair. Walter makes love with the singular focus of a lepidopterist skewering a butterfly with a pin. It is merciless, exacting sex—and yet there is a wonder in Walter's expression at odds with the implacable motion of his body, the heat of his mouth, his pitiless hands.

When he finds a way to make William cry out, the lines of his face grow soft, like a man enraptured by an aria. Like he has been moved by some great piece of art. Like *William* is a great piece of art. The way, perhaps, a lepidopterist might feel, capturing forever an exquisite expression of God's hand in the natural world.

When they finish Walter lies on his side, nose tucked beneath William's jaw and lips against William's throat, idly kissing, open-mouthed.

«If you're married,» he says, words loose and sloppy as his teeth graze tendons and his tongue tastes sweat, «and you're dying, what are you doing in Romania? What about your wife?»

William sighs.

«Is she so terrible?»

As he often does, William lets his silence answer for him.

«Do you even like women?» asks Walter.

«Some of them.»

Walter throws his head back and laughs, baring a flash of white skin beneath his clipped beard. «A politic answer.»

«It's true,» insists William, belligerent in Sue's defense. «I was…going to be married.»

«I thought you *were* married.»

Here it is his turn to laugh, though his laughter is less free. «Yes, but not to a woman I like.»

Walter squints up at him. «Why marry her, then?»

Why indeed? It seems hard to remember, now. Much harder than all the reasons he shouldn't have. All his friends told him not to do it, said she was a gold-digger and worse. Even his lawyer advised him to settle thirty pounds a year on her and wash his hands of the situation. With that and her husband's one thousand, she'd be comfortable. Why had it felt so necessary?

«We were…indiscreet,» he says. «There was a child. She swore her husband wouldn't divorce her, but…» He sighs. «And it looks good, doesn't it. For men like us.»

Walter exhales against his skin: short, sharp, amused. A swift, nauseating certainty comes over William: he's dangerously misjudged the situation. Ridiculous, with Walter naked in his bed, Walter kissing him on the street, but sometimes men think of themselves in a particular way. You never know what kinds of lies someone has told themselves.

Then Walter says, «If you worry about that sort of thing,» and presses the bridge of his nose into the soft skin under William's jaw.

The fear dissipates into annoyance, into envy. «Yes well, some of us have to.» And he always, always has. He's already alien in too many other ways; foreign born and shy, an orphan and a stammerer. Perhaps it's helped him in his writing, that distance, but it's kept him lonely, too. And even if Syrie had used him, he had used her too: to close that gap, to tightly stitch that gaping wound.

«Besides,» he says, «it was the right thing to do.»

«Was it?» Walter's teeth touch the tendon of his neck now, so he feels the transition between the two words as pressure, pain. Then a wet kiss, and a clarification: «If it has left you so unhappy, that you run away to die? What kind of husband is it who absconds like this?»

William looks down sharply, temper flaring. But Walter is already looking back with an amused, knowing expression. There is something almost girlish about it; William is reminded of the many actresses he's known. Of Sue.

«Why Jassy?» asks Walter, heavy-lidded, lips wet with spit William can still feel drying on his throat. «Why Romania, in the middle of a war? We could sign a treaty with the Germans tomorrow.»

Maybe it's foolish to do this now, but he is still smarting over Walter's tease. He wants to prove that what he's doing in Romania is more than running away. Prove it, perhaps, to both of them.

«I'm writing a series of articles for the *Times*,» he says, larding the well-practiced words with irony. And then, after a meaningful pause, «Officially.»

«And unofficially?»

«Unofficially, I am s…supposed to recruit you as an asset for the Secret Service Bureau.»

«Me?» Walter puts a theatrical hand to his chest. There is a heavy signet on his finger—gold—and it flashes in the darkness of the bedroom. «I can't imagine why.»

«I've heard a rumor,» says William. «That you can do the impossible.»

Walter's smile comes slow and feline; William thinks of Tenniel's Cheshire cat, all eyes and teeth. The illustration had scared him, as a child. Had scared Liza too.

«M. Maugham,» he says, «You would credit idle gossip?»

«I'm a writer,» says William. «And a spy. Where do you think I get my ideas?»

He won't agree to it, though. Not that night, nor the many nights that follow. William appeals to his patriotism—it's a fellow Romanian they're supposed to exfiltrate, after all. But he only asks, «Why me?»

William raises his eyebrows. He's read the notes in the file now, all of them. Silk stockings and chocolate for Maria Popescu. Foreign currency for fleeing refugees. Untainted food when there was typhus, cholera, anthrax during the bombing in Bucharest. His entire household, when the occupation started. When he confronts Walter with these facts, Walter waves them off.

«My household consists of one elderly butler and a cook.»

«And a collection of pictures worth fifteen million pounds.» William, letting his negotiation slide further toward flirtation. «You're a smuggler, M. Roşu.»

Walter snorts. «Is *that* what you think?»

«It's the obvious conclusion.»

Walter's jaw tenses, and he gives that Tenniel smile again. «Perhaps it is difficult for you to understand,» he says. «The obligations that I have to those under my protection.»

«Feudal,» says William, and it comes out a dirty word.

«Maybe,» says Walter, «but it is easier this way than to make promises I cannot keep. I like to pay my debts promptly and precisely, so that there are no surprises later.» Then, with stiletto accuracy, he says, «Perhaps this *is* something you can understand, given your… matrimonial straits. Would you not rather have paid her thirty pounds a year than sworn to love and cherish her?»

He doesn't remember giving Walter that precise figure. But there are some nights with Walter he doesn't remember his own name.

«Besides,» says Walter, «Even if I could do what you ask, I'm no longer a political man, and this stinks of politics.»

«And you owe your country nothing? You have no debts to pay on that score?» Walter has no service record, has never borne arms.

This lands badly, and receives a noble's sneer. «If anything, this country owes me.»

So William appeals to his honor as a gentleman and, when that fails, to his…baser natures.

«The parameters of my honor only extend so far.» It is a mild threat, made with a lingering glance that implies the penalty. Perhaps William does not appeal to Walter's baser natures so much as give in to his own.

After, he has to knot his necktie tightly, pulling his collar close to his throat. Walter has left a purple bruise on the column of his throat. The stiff edge of the linen doesn't quite cover it, but his muffler makes up the difference; and the raised collar of his coat.

He has been invited to dine at the French consul's house—one of the myriad strange social engagements offered to a foreign representative of the literati, once his presence in the city became known. The dining room is bright with gaslights and candles, the women's jewels glittering. To his delight, Madame Popescu is seated beside him, elegant in black velvet trimmed with jet.

«M. Maugham,» she says, and presses his hand. «What a pleasant surprise.»

He presses back. «Indeed.» He means it. «How is your daughter?»

«She's playing Bach now. Endless variation on a theme. She's very talented but, to speak frankly, I'm glad to be out of the house for a few hours.»

He laughs, as she means him to, and she watches him as he does. Her attention flickers, candlelight shivering in her gaze, and he sees her notice the shadow at the edge of his collar. Sees the powered lines at the corners of her eyes grow taut.

«And you?» she asks. «Have you spoken with M. Roşu?»

He swallows against the rigid starch of his collar, the knot of his tie. «Yes, in fact. We've become...quite good friends.»

«I'm glad,» she says, simpering so that he doesn't quite believe her. «I worried he would not answer my letter; he can be...difficult sometimes. Distant. Even with his friends.»

«He has not been so with me.»

«Hm.» He can't parse the meaning of the sound: assessment, envy, amusement? The light reflects from her eyes the same way it reflects from the jet collar at her throat, the thousands of tiny beads on her gown.

Finally she looks away, smoothing her napkin. «I haven't seen him in some time,» she says. «Perhaps the two of you would do me the honor of dining with my daughter and me.»

As if they are more than two bachelor gentlemen she happens to know, who might fill seats. As if they are the kind of people one invites to dinner as a unit. As if Mme. Popescu knows more than he might wish.

She glances back at him, and now there is the edge of mischief in her gaze. Malice, even. «Next week, perhaps?»

☦

THEY ARRIVE SEPARATELY, and yet by some twist of fate, Walter appears silently at William's elbow just as he rings the bell. He starts, and is still staring helplessly at Walter when the maid opens the door. William clears his throat and tucks his chin.

«Please wait, messieurs,» says the maid, and disappears.

«Good evening Willie.» Sleek and amused, on the surface Walter seems familiar. But there is tension in the line of his well-brushed shoulders and glossy silk lapels.

«Are you…all right?»

«Quite,» he says, too sincerely.

Mme. Popescu is artfully harried when she greets them, the charming picture of a hostess spinning many plates. It's a trifle overdone, for a party so small. Like Walter, her demeanor has a stagey, hollow quality. Amateurish. Christmas pantomime.

«My daughter isn't feeling well,» says Mme. Popescu, which goes some way toward explaining her distraction, although not far enough. «I'm afraid it will just be us.»

An unbalanced table that only a wealthy widow could get away with, and that only in a time of war. The whole thing looks very odd indeed. But it's an odd time in Jassy—an odd time in the world, unprecedented—and he has gathered that Mme. Popescu is a bit odd herself.

«Brandy?» she asks, leading them into the drawing room. She pours. Walter drifts to the fireplace and stretches his hands out toward the blaze. They are long hands, but not slender. The bones and veins stand out beneath the skin.

«M. Maugham?» Mme. Popescu is offering him a glass. William realizes he has been staring. He wonders if she realizes it too.

«Thank you.» He takes the brandy, drinks. «And thank you for the invitation.»

«Thank *you* for the excuse,» she says. Then, slightly louder, not to William but past his shoulder: «I think M.

Roşu has been avoiding me.»

Walter, backlit and looming by the fire, takes offense. «Maria, I heard that.»

Her laughter is satiny: a sensual, slippery sound. Intimate, like his use of her Christian name. But that intimacy is tinged with bitterness. William's writer's sense, honed by years of observation, catches the thread of something old and unforgiven.

What *is* this dinner party? Some entrée to blackmail? An ill-conceived revenge? Is Mme. Popescu just nosy? William feels suddenly tired—this is the sort of scenario he likes to write, not the kind he likes to find himself caught up in. He's had enough of that, thank you.

Walter separates from the shadows like viscous liquid, like a bubble of black mercury, and slides to where William and Mme. Popescu stand by the sideboard. Once he is in better light, William realizes how sinister he appeared in the darkness.

«Perhaps I have been avoiding you.» Walter pours himself a glass of brandy. «You are a strong-willed woman and your company can become…demanding.»

«Can you blame me for making a few demands?» She busies herself checking her watch, winding it, but even with her face turned down William can see her eyes turn hard and flashing, like her mourning jet. «I know what you can do, and what do I get? Chocolates. Silk stockings.»

Walter stills, his fingers loosely ringing the neck of the crystal decanter. When he speaks his tone is carefully light. Precarious. «You didn't say no to them.»

When Mme. Popescu looks up, she has mastered whatever emotion William glimpsed. She lays her hand on his arm and when she speaks she is gay again, though it is a caustic gaiety, the kind of thing he's heard from actresses, old fairies. The gaiety of the wounded. «He's a good friend until you need something,» she says. «And then you won't see him for months.»

William is struck with an irrational conviction that Mme. Popescu knows what he has asked Walter to do. Wonders if perhaps Max did approach her first.

But no. She is not looking at William like a conspirator. She is looking at him in a way that makes him think of Syrie: a woman who feels hard done by. A woman asking for his sympathy, or maybe something more. Revenge, then. It sets his teeth on edge to be so used, but it also piques his curiosity.

«I hope that's not true,» he says, acquiescing to the drama and the intrigue. Her grip on his arm tightens. «I recently asked a f…» It jams.

«A favor?» She finishes for him. «Oh dear.»

A sharp sound makes them both jump. Walter has jammed the stopper back into the decanter: the crack of heavy glass on glass.

«I do have my own interests to protect,» says Walter.

«Yes,» says Mme. Popescu. Her fingers on William's arm are like manacles. They pinch. «A skill that comes so naturally to you, which the rest of us have had to learn very quickly of late.»

Walter catches William's eye and smiles grimly. «Not all of us,» he says.

THE DINNER MME. Popescu serves is not as lavish as the food that Walter has served William. She's found a slice of mutton somewhere, but it's tough and lean and her cook hasn't been able to make much of it. There are plenty of potatoes. Soup with thin, sour broth. Walter eats well, William moderately, and Mme. Popescu hardly at all. She watches them both with more than a hostess's usual attention, like she is searching for more bruises, watching for a tell.

She knows, she knows, William thinks, silently pleading with Walter for discretion. Every so often Walter gives him the ghost of a smile, as if he can tell what tired script is running around inside William's head.

So what? the smile seems to say. What William wouldn't give to care so little.

«How are you finding Jassy?» Mme. Popescu asks him, picture book polite hostess.

«It's…beautiful,» says William.

«Yes,» she says, and he hears the acid start to leak. «Very. But, as M. Roşu has no doubt told you, not as beautiful as Bucharest.»

Walter sets down his knife. «Your tongue is very sharp tonight, Mme. Popescu.» His tone is tolerant, amused.

«Forgive me,» she says, not sounding sincere. «It has been whetted by my day.»

Walter goes back to his tough meat, as though he hasn't heard the invitation. But William, who has already played into her schemes once tonight, feels the onus to sustain conversation. «How so, madame?»

«Did you enjoy my daughter's piano playing?» she asks. «My little musical afternoon?»

«Of course,» he says, though he remembers very little of what Mlle. Popescu played. It's the right thing to say, and it doesn't matter anyway—it isn't the point of the question. He's only setting her up for her next line.

«Well not everyone did.» She pauses, drinks some wine. «I had a note from an old friend, a friend who refused her invitation but nevertheless knew every detail of the party.» Light shivers on the surface of the wine; she's smiling, but her hand isn't steady.

«Apparently I should still be shut up alone inside my house, curtains drawn. Didn't you know, sharing Ana's music is an affront to my husband's memory.» She sets down her glass too hard and splashes the white linen tablecloth with red. Drawing an unsteady breath, she puts a hand over the stain and says softly: «Iacob loved to hear her play.»

Old mourning rituals have been made almost impossible by the scale of death at the front. But in times like these, some people find comfort in clinging to tradition. And perhaps especially in scorning others for discarding it. He begins to revise his suspicions; perhaps there is no ulterior motive here. Perhaps Mme. Popescu is simply scrambling for sympathetic company. But that doesn't explain Walter's unease.

«She was upset at the impropriety,» says William, «but not about the Germans?»

«Oh of *course* she was upset about the Germans!» Mme. Popescu waves the maid to refill her glass—a maid, and not a footman, another impropriety, just like this dinner party, but it must be hard to find young men to fill domestic positions, even with the army demobbed. «We are *all* upset about the Germans. But they're here and they're likely to stay for God only knows how long, so we had all better get used to them.»

«Nothing lasts forever,» says Walter, almost to himself.

Mme. Popescu stares sourly at her plate. «I suppose you would know.»

Lovers, then, and Walter must have ended it. So much for his theory about sympathetic company.

«How fortunate you are, M. Roşu,» she says, «that circumstances have not made you cynical. But then, circumstances have hardly imposed themselves on you to any great degree.»

«I would not count myself lucky,» he says.

«Ah yes, the bombings in Bucharest.» Mme. Popescu widens her eyes in mock sympathy. «How horrible, to escape with only your fortune and your paintings and your French cook.» The false sympathy falls away. «What the rest of us would give for your misfortune.»

«Maria,» he says, in a voice that William has never

heard him use. His boyar's voice, William thinks: cold and unyielding, an iron door with violence locked behind it.

But Mme. Popescu sneers and says to William, «You know Walter hasn't served? Not at the front, or behind the lines, not even in an office.»

Of course. She's *jealous.* The realization fills him with pity. She is hurting herself for a chance to embarrass Walter in front of William. It won't work—he's known about Walter's service record since he first got a look at that file in Max's office. But he can hardly tell Mme. Popescu, under the circumstances. So he says nothing: only widens his eyes at her, and then looks down the table at Walter.

«Regrettably,» he says, «I have a condition which makes military service impossible.»

The statement has the rhythm of practice; William should recognize it, as so many of his own statements follow the same cadence.

«I'm sorry,» he says, wondering what condition it could be. Walter has seemed in perfect health since the day they met.

Mme. Popescu snorts into her wine. «Don't be. He doesn't deserve your pity.»

THEY DON'T LINGER over coffee. Mme. Popescu pleads her sick daughter. William is glad to leave. Outside, the night is bitter, the stars crystalline in the sky. The cold is so dry that William's breath doesn't even fog. That breath comes more easily than it might, but he doesn't trust the ease of it.

«What on *earth?*» he asks, half of Walter, half of the universe at large.

«Forgive Maria,» says Walter. «I deserve most of what she said.»

His driver is bringing the car around—William wonders what kinds of petrol restrictions are in place, but doesn't wonder much about how Walter skirts them.

«You were lovers, and it ended badly.» William meets his eyes. «*You* ended it, badly.»

Walter's smile is ironic. He says nothing.

«I didn't understand what I was asking her to do,» says William, «when I asked for the introduction. I'm amazed she agreed. I'm amazed you accepted.»

«Maria has a keen sense for what will pique my interest,» says Walter. «It's what I liked about her, from the beginning.»

«And what *does* pique your interest?» asks William, letting a little of his own pique through. It has not been a pleasant evening.

A wry twist to Walter's mouth. «The unconventional.»

«Well she certainly is that.»

«She likes to try to make me feel uncomfortable,» he says.

«Does she ever succeed?»

Walter's expression is enigmatic. He doesn't answer the question. «I apologize that she brought you into it. Perhaps she sees you as a new weapon in her arsenal.»

He doesn't like the sound of that. «Is she discreet, Mme. Popescu?»

That makes Walter laugh, but he sounds tired. «She can be, certainly.»

It is not reassuring. «Do you trust her?»

Walter really looks at him then, and William sees the realization come into his eyes. «Willie, be easy. You have nothing to fear from that quarter. Not from her.»

«You *do* trust her,» he says. Then relief makes way for indignation. «But you treated her abominably!»

«As you say.» Walter checks his watch. «We *were* lovers.

But no longer. May I drive you home?»

William, galled, ignores the offer. «And you don't feel you owe her some sympathy? Some civility, even? Or do you feel like you've bought her off with silk stockings and chocolates? Paid your debt?»

«My thirty pounds a year,» says Walter, to the gutter. The bitterness of his smile warps it into a grimace.

«You do feel some responsibility for her, then.»

Walter's shrug is cramped, denying. «Perhaps.»

«You feel guilty,» William says, surprised. He should stop pushing, but it's heady to have some insight into Walter's character at last. Some small foothold in his sleek façade. «You treated her badly because you're ashamed.»

Walter rounds on him, snarling wordlessly. That iron door unlocked. William flinches, throws up an arm. By the time he's realized Walter isn't going to strike him, Walter has slammed the door of his car and it's pulling away from the steps of Mme. Popescu's house.

So there is the answer to his question: Mme. Popescu succeeds in making Walter very uncomfortable indeed.

"He won't do it," William tells Max, before pleasantries. Max no longer looks like a man who wants to offer them, if he ever did. There are fewer stacks of paper in his office now, and many more boxes, neatly packed.

"Maugham," says Max, and nods in the direction of the empty chair at his desk. William drops into it, suddenly aware of his own exhaustion. With Walter, he has been exerting himself more than he should. Now, in the cold light of day in Max's freezing office, faced with the war and all its consequences, including those of his failure, his illness punishes him for his negligence.

"He won't do it," says William again. "Doesn't get involved in politics."

Max's scowl has grown familiar.

"Besides, he says it's impossible."

"That's what they all say, until you've added enough zeroes to the end of your offer."

William shook his head. "What does he need with m…m…?"

"Money? Suppose you're right. What would sway him?"

William shrugs heavily; it feels like there's a cold, wet blanket draped across his back. He realizes he has sweated straight through his shirt. What would sway Walter? Not money or honor or patriotism. Not even blackmail. He seems to be divorced from every sense of obligation or enticement.

Except, William realizes, one very particular shame.

"I don't know," he says, thoughtful, testing the edges of that idea, wondering if Walter's guilt can be made transitive. "Maybe…the girl?"

Max makes a face. "The *human* element, is it? Fine." He unlocks one of his desk drawers and snaps irritably through a rank of files until he finds the one he's after.

William wonders if Max was ever any good at his job, ever took pleasure in it. After all, what is intelligence gathering but the human element? It's human right the way through.

"There she is," says Max, and drops the file in front of him. "Another bloody Maria, though this one's more on the Magdalene side."

A young woman's mugshot: hair in a messy pompadour, dark blonde or light brown. Huge pale eyes. Narrow shoulders that slope away to nothing. *Moraru, Maria. Place of Birth: Bucharest. Date of Birth: 1897. Profession: Prostitute.*

"Pretty," says William, and wonders if her name will help his case with Walter.

"Older than that now," says Max. "That's a drunk and disorderly or whatever they call it here, from a few years back. She was rounded up during the occupation, with the rest of her sisterhood. Did you know about this?"

William shakes his head. She is very young. He would not have thought twenty one—or even twenty—was so young, when he was that age. Now she seems like a child.

"The Germans herded them all up to some barracks in Mizil, cleaned them up, gave them all their shots. At the expense of the state. Sounds like Christian charity, doesn't it? Well, you can imagine what they wanted them for."

And he can well imagine what she might have picked up inside a German army barracks that might be useful to the British government. "She's back in Bucharest?"

"Either that or we're going to send an agent into a tidy little trap, aren't we?"

"Can I read the message?"

Max waves a dismissive hand at the file. "It's in there, along with the rest of her transmissions. What good it'll do you with Roşu, I can't imagine."

Max, thinks William, seems to suffer from a dearth of imagination.

"Sweet Jesus," he says, as if to confirm William's summing up. "I can't wait to get back to Blighty and a decent cup of tea."

Maria Moraru makes for nostalgic reading. She reminds him of his days at St. Thomas, clerking in the Out Patients clinic and coming face to face with the Lambeth poor. The same litany of destitution and tragedy, sharply limned by a furious blaze of pride.

Native of Bucharest; fifth of seven children, five of them girls; left home at fourteen to marry a man who subsequently disappeared. Worked in a factory for a few years, turned to prostitution aged seventeen—maybe sixteen. He wonders idly about her birthday. Two children, or maybe only one—belonging to whom? The husband? He's long gone—never mentioned again beyond the first acknowledgement of their existence. Where are they now? And how much of this is true, anyway? There are contradictions in the story, noted by her handler.

But oh, she shrieks off the page. Never mind her mug shot is monochrome, he can see her in full living color. London color, maybe, but aren't things the same everywhere, in their way? She'll have a smart mouth, not to mention filthy. She'll be clever, and every edge of her will be sharp as a razor blade. Her reports are rich with detail, albeit colored by strong opinions her handler shouldn't have taken the trouble to encode. William laughs at a few, and sees why he did.

She's a good agent, even if she needs a firm hand–an agent he wouldn't be ashamed to run. Max doesn't know what he's got with Maria.

Never having met her, he likes her, in the way he likes things that fascinate him. He likes her like he liked Sadie Thompson, the prostitute who fled Hawai'i on the same cramped boat with him and Gerald, who drove the missionaries crazy with her parties and her phonograph and her commerce with the crew. He likes Maria because he imagines that around her, all kinds of things might happen. And human drama is his stock in trade.

He likes her because, like Walter, his interest is piqued by the unconventional.

He leaves the consulate after reading through the file, twice. Doesn't take any notes, which is a shame; he'll remember most of it but he likes to think through things with a pen in his hand. Still, security.

She makes him want to write, Maria and her unconventionality. He's got a couple of stories he's poking at, South Pacific stories, one of them about Sadie Thompson. In the whirlwind of courting Walter, worrying about the outcome of his venture for Max, he's set his notebooks aside.

Now he goes back to his plain little flat and settles at the desk in the sitting room. The afternoon shadows are long, and even the south-facing window has gone dark by this time of day.

When he sits, the weight of his body catches up to him. The cold settles more deeply into his bones. His chest aches and his fever begins to creep up from wherever it sleeps inside of him. His pen touches the paper and rests there, ink spreading from the nib in a black corona.

Green palms, he thinks to himself. Grass houses. White churches and the breathless, stifling heat. The whore and the missionary and the unending rattle of rain on the corrugated iron roof.

All that will come is the cold, and his exhaustion. His worry for Gerald, which has grown quiet of late, comes surging back. Gerald, there with him in the rain and the heat and gone now, who knows where. It's the not knowing that's the worst, because the line is still open. A tenuous connection stretched over continents with only static at the end.

It costs less to be alone. But he can't cut the line. Not to Gerald. Not even to Syrie and Liza, despite himself. He can't shake Maria Popescu's grip on his arm. Maria Moraru. Walter.

A draft brings up goosebumps under his clothes. He lets the pen fall, forgets to cap it. Ink spatters across the page. It is of vital importance that he get to bed, and by the time he's gotten there he's burning hot. He sheds his clothes and crawls beneath the covers, shivering. The last vestiges of twilight fade into night and he sleeps, or thinks he does.

He dreams of Syrie. Maybe. He cannot tell if it is a dream, or memory, or pure hallucination.

She is here, in Jassy, the way she is always chasing him, always opening his door, always finding him when he doesn't want to be found. She is redecorating the dingy flat, and she has replaced all of the furniture with horrible pink and white poufs and topped every table with ugly gold-glazed porcelain figurines. She has left Liza behind in London, alone, and won't tell William who is taking care of her or how she is.

"If you want to know," she says, "You must come home and see her." And then, "If you don't come home I'll tell the papers all about you and that American boy. I'll tell them what you do on Capri. If you thought the divorce case was a scandal in the papers, just you wait. I'll ruin you."

Gerald comes as if she'd called him: rakish grin, sandy hair, smoking a cigarette and unbuttoning his uniform jacket with one hand. The buttons flash as they pop from the holes, tantalizing as a music hall burlesque. But when the lapels fall open they show a grisly wound. The kind of thing William treated on the front, the kind of hole that shells and shrapnel made in flesh, the kind of thing that meant all you could do was hold a man's hand like he was a child, while he cried helplessly for his mother like children do.

Then Sue is there, her cool hand on his brow while he cries just as helplessly. He knows she isn't real, knows the hand is just a cold draft, the warmth of her body through the blankets just his own fever reflected back. But it is so good to see her that he lets himself believe.

"You got married," he says. It sounds petulant, and it sounds like somebody else is saying it.

She only smiles and strokes his brow. She is wearing a loose shift and nothing else, luscious curves beneath fine muslin. She is pregnant, he realizes. Her belly is round and ripe and he wants to smooth his palm across it.

"I was going to ask you," he says. "Even so." And he would have, happily. Not the grudging acceptance of his situation with Syrie. "You didn't have to say yes to him. I would have said it was mine. Even if it didn't look like me. I would have loved it, as much as I love Liza. More."

If he had married Sue, there would not have been a Liza, or any of the tragicomic circumstances surrounding her conception and birth and bastard early years. They could have been generous with each other. He knew she was apt to stray, and loved her anyway; just like she knew about Harry, and Capri. She might have liked Gerald. She would never have threatened him with blackmail like he fears Syrie might.

She pets his hair, puts her fingertips to his tears. His sobs subside into racking, bloody coughs. When he's finally able to draw breath it's Walter there, sitting on the bed where Sue had been, his hand as cool as hers but firmer, pressing William's skull into the pillow.

He leans down and kisses William—a strange and hungry kiss. First the fullness of his lower lip, which Walter sucks into his mouth like an oyster, like escargot coming from a shell. His tongue presses against William's bottom teeth, his gums, sliding with muscular insistence first along one side of his jaw and then the other, all the way to his molars. Then under his own tongue, and on top of it, invasive. Curling against the slender ribbon of skin between his two front teeth, pushing it taut so that sensation zings up the front of William's face and follows the nerves down his spine to his groin.

Walter follows the curve of his upper teeth, front and back, flattens his tongue against William's hard palate and licks it. Catches William's upper lip in a delicate bite and holds it softly, though William has the sense he is restraining himself. There is a shivering quality to his delicacy that speaks of great force barely restrained.

When he draws away his mouth is red with blood. It is smeared across his lips and disappearing into his beard. His teeth are red. There is a smudge of red on the tip of his nose.

"Did I hemorrhage?" asks William. "Am I dying?"

He is used to Walter's expression softening for him, used to a laugh that is more sigh, more exhalation. He is used to the deepening of the lines around Walter's eyes, the rise of his mustache when he smiles.

But Walter's face remains immobile as carved white limestone, like something decorating a crypt. Only his eyes move. A faint sliver of light slides over their dark surfaces as Walter watches his face. "You are all dying, William. And it has been a long time since I cared."

Even in his stillness—perhaps because of it—it's clear that he's upset. "I'm sorry," William says.

Walter flows forward in a single movement, his body moving like a cat's does, inside its skin. His arms bracket William's shoulders, hands plunged deep into the duvet. The force of his descent has loosed a single feather, which curls past in William's peripheral vision. An odd detail for a fever dream, crisp with specificity.

"You," says Walter, close to William's face. "At Maria's dinner. You almost… you made me want to…"

"Care," says William, watching Walter's bloody mouth. His lips are parted slightly, showing the edges of his teeth.

Walter makes a low, desiring sound and falls on him: not to kiss, this time, though at first it is a hot open mouth on William's throat, the curl of Walter's eager tongue. And then, good lord it hurts.

Until it doesn't. His head swims, lolling on the pillow away from the slick cushion of Walter's hair. He can feel the roll of Walter's working jaw, his rhythmic swallowing, feel a thread of his own blood that has escaped to run down his neck and trace the curve of his shoulder, disappearing into the bedclothes. He feels pleasantly warm, dizzy, the world at a muffled distance. His arousal stirs, languorous, and he closes his eyes. The blackness in his head is the deep pile of plush velvet. He gives up and falls into its luxury.

When he wakes, his fever is gone and his chest feels free: no iron band of pain obstructing his breath. The bedroom is still murky but there is sun streaming into the sitting room; the door is open and he can see motes of dust in the ray of light. He lies quiet for a moment, feeling curiously buoyant, not quite tethered to the earth. He watches a few flakes of snow sift down the air shaft, bright against the sooty bricks.

After a while, he turns over. The bedroom sways like a ship, and he steadies himself with a hand pressed into the mattress.

There is a single spot of rusty brown on the sheets.

Familiar enough. Hasn't he woken to spots like this before? Left them on his handkerchiefs, his shirtfronts, his collars and cuffs? Of course it was all a dream. He didn't stammer once, the whole time.

IT'S THE HUNGER that gets him out of bed. He's ravenous. His small larder yields a bit of stale bread and hard cheese, which calms the spinning of his head. He dresses and goes out for coffee and donuts, dreaming of beefsteak, kidneys, chops.

The sun is hard in the cloudless sky, the shadows crisp and the white stones of the buildings blinding. William takes a deep breath of scouring winter air: coal smoke, dirty snow, the ache of cold. He lets it out. Takes another. Takes great gulping breaths, again and again, and doesn't cough. He wants to run down the middle of the street, lungs working like bellows, and feel the pounding of his heart in his ears.

The doctor told him, when he was first diagnosed, that this was common with consumptives. The spikes of fever and chills, the weakness and exhaustion, would come and go.

In between he might feel better than he had in weeks; better than he'd ever felt. *Hectic* was the word he used.

"Don't over-exert yourself," he cautioned. "You'll pay the price for it in the end."

But it feels so *good*. Without the fever sweat his clothes are dry and warm. His breath is free, his blood is up. He feels like he could do anything.

At the café down the block, the one that has become his regular, he gets his little cup of coffee, his plate of donuts, and on a whim, a glass of white-hot clear plum brandy. He drinks it in one gulp, a challenge to himself, and though it burns going down it doesn't make him cough. He smiles at the empty tumbler.

«Never saw an Englishman smile like that at a glass of țuică.»

The voice is familiar, with its schoolboy French. The face too: heavy good looks.

«Mihai,» the young man reminds him. «I have seen you here often. But you prefer to write.»

«Not today,» says William.

«Good news?» asks Mihai, and sits down beside William, uninvited.

William shakes his head.

«Fine weather?»

William shrugs.

«Right,» says Mihai. «You don't talk much.»

«I…» He makes a fist, grits his teeth, prays for the words to come. After an airless pause, they burst out in a rush: «I have a stammer.»

Mihai's smile is a slow one. It rolls across his face like jam on the back of a spoon. «Oh,» he says. «Well. We don't have to talk at all.»

He's so bold. William wishes he could ever manage this, the leap of faith that follows all the careful assessment, all the calculation. But. He can do the next best thing. He can take the last bite of his donut, finish his coffee, and meet Mihai's challenging gaze. He can tip his head slightly to the door, fold his napkin, drop some coins on the counter to cover what he owes.

«I HAVE A D…DINNER engagement,» says William, hours later, when the sun has set. «I think.»

Mihai laughs at him. «You think?» He reaches down to fish tobacco and papers from the pocket of his coat.

William watches as he rolls a meager cigarette: his thick fingers with their blunt nails, the pink flicker of his tongue as he licks the paper. «I…quarreled with my host.»

Mihai snorts and opens the drawer of William's bedside table without asking. What's in it? William hasn't even looked, in all the time he's been here. He realizes how lightly he's been living in his flat.

Whatever he finds Mihai is unsatisfied, and leans down again to retrieve his book of matches. Striking one, he releases a sharp scent of sulfur into the air. He breathes out a cloud of smoke. William inhales. No tickle, no catch. The scent of tobacco reminds him of the cadaver room at medical school, where they all smoked like chimneys to cover the smell of the formaldehyde. Is it morbid, that he finds the memory comforting?

«How bad was it? The fight.» Mihai offers him the cigarette. William takes a drag, but mostly holds the smoke in his mouth. He doesn't want to push his luck. He begins to assemble his evening dress.

«Bad, then.» Mihai smiles at the cigarette when William hands it back, then puts it into his mouth and talks around it. «The host,» he says. «He's a friend?»

The way he says it means *this* kind of friend. The kind that smokes naked in your bed. William pays close attention to pushing the studs through his shirtfront.

«I'm not jealous,» Mihai says.

«No,» says William. «Of course.»

«Why did you fight?»

«I need a favor,» William says. It isn't exactly the truth. But it's the larger, contextual truth. It is the only fight Walter seems to have with anyone.

«Money?» Mihai asks.

If only it were that easy. «No. I—» he can't explain. But: «I n…need him to do something for me. He won't. So I m…must figure out how to convince him.»

«Money,» says Mihai again, this time half-joking. It does make William laugh, and he takes a few of the silly war-time postage-stamp notes from his billfold. Mihai folds them into his matchbook.

«He's very wealthy,» William says. «But…lonely, I think.» Then it occurs to him: «Perhaps determined to remain so.»

Why should it hurt, to realize this? Why does it feel like a rejection? Walter is an asset. A friend of circumstance. A foreign affair. It isn't William's business if he wants to cloak himself in misery and die alone. Yes misery—because it might cost less to be alone, but what miser ever rejoiced in his circumstances, at the end? William certainly isn't rejoicing much in his own.

Mihai sucks thoughtfully at the dwindling butt of his fag. «And you want to change his mind.»

«About the favor, yes.»

Exhaling smoke, Mihai says with certainty: «About the loneliness.»

William remembers the dangerous furrow between Walter's brows, at the mere implication he could be lonely. His arch cruelty toward Mme. Popescu, his shame, take on a new dimension. She still loves him, and he wants to keep her at arm's length, if not further. He is ashamed not only because he has treated her badly, but perhaps because he does not, in his heart, *want* to.

William finishes with his studs, his cufflinks. As he knots his tie he ponders different approaches. He thinks of the furrow between Walter's brows, his parting snarl at Mme. Popescu's, and wonders: anger, or pain?

He fastens his waistcoat and slips on his tails.

«You look like a waiter,» Mihai says. Then, flirtatious: «A handsome waiter.» He taps the ash from his cigarette into the tooth glass William has left by the bed.

«Stay as long as you like,» says William.

«No thanks,» says Mihai, already getting up to leave. «I also have a *dinner engagement*. I don't just think. I know.»

On the threshold of Walter's Brâncovenesc mansion, William marshals his nerves. He has received no note rescinding his invitation, but perhaps Walter imagines that he doesn't need to send one, not after that.

But the majordomo comes to the door when he rings, and lets him in, and shows him to the drawing room, where Walter is drinking plum brandy—better than the stuff they serve in the café.

When they're alone, William says: «I wasn't sure if I should come.»

«Of course you should have,» Walter says. He rises from his chair and goes to the sideboard. When he turns around his expression is well-schooled. «I apologize. I behaved badly.»

William doesn't deny it. He takes the glass Walter gives him and drinks. Thinned by fumes, the pungent scent of ripe plums rises transparent from the liquor like the ghost of some long-ago summer.

«I'm glad,» says Walter, haltingly. «That you did. Come.»

William looks up from his drink, surprised at this admission. The reluctance of it reminds him of his dream:

of Walter's unfinished sentence, of William finishing it for him.

He catches Walter's eye and Walter looks away, nose in the air. He isn't blushing, but every fiber of him looks as though he should be.

«I'm glad too,» he says, and Walter's posture relaxes fractionally.

When dinner is served it is the beefsteak he has craved all day, rare enough to bleed. He thinks of Mme. Popescu's stringy mutton. *What the rest of us would give for your misfortune.*

«How long did you stay in Bucharest?» asks William. «Were you there for the bombings?»

«No,» says Walter. «But I did return, after. As you know.»

He lets the snipe pass by. «Was the damage very bad?»

A pause, as Walter considers the untouched meat on his plate, glistening in its bloody sauce. «I have never seen anything like it.»

Who has? Nothing in history compares to any part of this war. Nor anything in imagination. It beggars belief daily. «I'm sorry.»

Walter inclines his head, then steers the conversation elsewhere. But although he keeps up his end, trotting out amusing anecdotes and asking the right questions at the right times, he seems distracted, pensive. He barely touches his precious beef. William wonders if Florea, the manservant, will sell it on the sly.

After dinner they adjourn to the library. There is a fire already burning in the hearth, the lamps low and warm against the burgundy silk that covers the walls above the wainscoting. The books in their shelves flicker in and out of shadow, the gilded ribs of their spines gleaming intermittently. Walter nods toward one of the deep English-style armchairs by the fireplace and goes to pour them each a glass of cognac. All wordless, but not waiting.

There is an air of control to his silence; it is not William's to break.

When William is seated, crystal balloon cupped in his hands, Walter does not take the other chair. He sets his cognac down untouched and goes to the window, drawing aside the heavy drapes. There is a full moon, brighter even than the firelight and low gas lamps. It makes his starched shirtfront gleam, catches in the silver that threads through his beard.

«Did you ever go to Bucharest?» he asks. «Before the war?"

«No.»

«A pity. I like Bucharest. She is always changing. But then, so is the rest of the world. Changing, changing, and somehow still the same.»

«Even with the war?»

At that Walter looks away, out the window. The snowy moonlight turns his pale face plaster white. The motion fades from him, like dust settling as the wind dies. He stands there in perfect stillness, looking like a model in a waxworks. Like a corpse posed for a Victorian mourning album. When he speaks it makes William jump. As if the waxworks doll had suddenly blinked, the corpse drawn breath.

«Bucharest,» he says, «has been sacked by Janissaries, leveled by fires and earthquakes, decimated by plague. Occupied by the Habsburgs, the Russians, the Greeks. Torn apart by her own people on many occasions. And yet, the lindens have bloomed every spring.» His voice, his gaze, are far away, perhaps under those very same lindens. «This is the first year in many that I have doubted them.»

«I don't think the Kaiser can s…stop the trees from flowering,» says William, but Walter is shaking his head. And William knows what he means. It isn't about the lindens.

«The first mention of Bucharest,» says Walter, «the first historical record we have? They call it *my* city. My city, and I did not feel *safe* there.»

He says this so vehemently that William almost misses the impossibility. He is still grappling with the implications when Walter adds, more softly:

«I do not know if I will feel safe again anywhere.»

«The f…» William stops, licks his lips. Swallows hard. «When would that be, exactly?»

Walter's smile is the slow movement of shadow across a sculpture, the illusion of expression. «September twentieth, fourteen fifty nine.»

William thinks that he must have heard wrong. He moves his jaw to pop his ears. He watches Walter's eyes as they lose their focus again, reflect the moon.

«A very good season for the grape harvest, in that part of the world. The wines put down, they said, would grow better and better for years.»

«You can't possibly expect me…» But William finds he can't go on. Not because of his stammer. Because Walter has gone still again, even moreso than before. His chest does not rise or fall. He stares out the window with his hand on the drapes and he might as well be marble, obsidian set into the sockets of his eyes. It is the stillness of a monument. A tomb.

But he has also seen how Walter can move: the inhuman swiftness of him, the startling strength. Like—like a cat twisting inside its own skin. But that had been a dream, hadn't it?

His hand is at his throat before he can check the motion, fingertips touching his high starched collar, the nubbled pique of his tie.

Walter catches the tic, laughs a little, lets the drapes fall shut. «I am surprised that you remember. You were babbling to an empty room when I arrived.»

William gets out of his chair, the wild strength of his own heartbeat strangling him. He knocks over the cognac in his haste and the liquor soaks the bearskin laid before the hearth.

Walter watches him, amused. Maybe his lack of concern should frighten William more. Instead, he feels ashamed, and the shame makes him angry. He stands straight, breathing hard through his nose, and stares Walter down. «What did you do to me?»

This time Walter's smile is no shadow. It is a moon of its own: crescent, gleaming, cold. «Would you like me to do it again?»

It is very different, to go knowingly into…whatever this is. To soberly follow Walter up the shadowed curves of his staircase, under the flickering eyes of dozens of half-lit oil paintings. William's hand keeps rising to his collar, until he balls it into a fist and presses it to his side. He is remembering the pain.

But after, bliss. The darkness of deep sleep, untroubled by dreams. And then, perhaps, another good day. And another. As many good days as he has nights with Walter.

The bedroom is dark and cold—no fire here. William shivers, which might be the temperature, or fear. This is so very foolish. What is he doing here? What *is* Walter? He could kill him, and then what about Liza?

What *about* Liza? He came to Romania to die. And this seems preferable to consumption or the war.

Walter takes William's hand in his, and his palm is icy cold. The chill of the windowpane lingers against his lapels and shirtfront, unwarmed, William realizes, by any human heartbeat, any flow of blood. There has always been a fire, or a radiator, or they have been in public and they have not touched in any way that would have told him that the warmth of Walter's skin did not come from within.

Then Walter kisses him. A real kiss, not the hungry invasions that have clearly been his way of making do:

hors d'oeuvres. He is unhurried, luxurious, not overly thorough. Like a man who has made a long study of the art. A man who isn't very worried about the passage of time.

William has never been kissed like this, not by a man. Even on Capri, even in private, there was a certain self-consciousness, a sixth sense for watching eyes. Gerald came the closest, but that was purely down to bravado, or sometimes down to drink. Walter kisses like he doesn't care. And why would he, after nearly five hundred years?

But the kiss is merely an amuse-bouche. When William's collar springs loose from its studs, Walter draws a sharp breath through his nose. He licks the groove beneath William's jawbone with deliberate care, and when he pulls away William can feel the chill across the hot beating of his own pulse. Between William's legs Walter pauses for a long time, tracing the map of veins inside his thigh with fingers and tongue. William has never been so aware of the circulatory system. Not in the surgery, not in his exams. Femoral superficial, Femoral profunda, anastomotica magna. Walter follows the paths of his arteries unerringly.

«Can you…» says William, dry mouthed. «Does it need to be the neck?»

Walter's head comes up, and though his face doesn't flush, his lips don't darken, and his black eyes don't show a bloom, the desire is written so starkly across his features William feels like he can see a ghost of all the other signs. A phantom rush of blood.

And then he sinks his teeth into William's thigh.

To see him do it, wide awake, William flinches hard away—out of sheer instinct and memory of pain. Out of a sense of *wrongness*: abjection, disgust, and fear. But Walter's hands are on his leg, clamped like a vice above the knee and below the groin, and the flinch avails him nothing.

Then the pain begins to fade into warmth, and his head goes cottony and vague. Walter's hands on his leg soften, his grip shifting to knead into the muscle. The movement of his jaw, the sound of his swallowing, the oily smears of blood between his lips and William's skin…

William remembers the first time he opened his eyes to watch: the taboo of it, another person touching the parts of his body that shouldn't be touched, shouldn't be seen. The shock as their eyes met his, the impossibility of pretending. A voyeurism too immediate for safety. There was no page, no proscenium to contain the consequences.

Walter looks up. Mouth half-pressed to William's thigh, a mess of red and black—William can see the two deep punctures in his own skin, can watch as Walter presses his fingers past his own lips and touches the two holes, pushes just hard enough that William can feel the edges of the wounds stretch, willing. Then Walter sits up and puts his two bloody fingers to William's lips.

«You taste good,» he says, then leans in to put his mouth to William's throat.

William wakes in the middle of the night under layers of mink and goose down. There is a fire in the hearth casting unreliable light across the ceiling. Walter is sitting in bed beside him, on top of the covers, still naked but impervious to chill.

«Here,» he says, noticing—from what sign?—that William is awake. He takes a tea tray from the nightstand and settles it between them: a slice of dense honey cake filled with cheese and jam, a steaming pot of cocoa, a stiff pour of brandy.

William levers himself out from under the covers: an immense effort that makes his head spin. The cocoa smells incredible. It pours thickly, made with the heavy cream cafés can no longer find. And though William knows it is just money—surely it is just money?—he cannot shake the image of Walter creeping like a witch's familiar into the buttery. Like a rat, Max said.

«You're not a smuggler,» says William. He opens his eyes again and meets the gaze of his reflection in the highly polished copper of the tray. His is the only face reflected there.

Walter's laughter is motion more than sound. «What am I, then?»

He could borrow words from Stoker, Polidori, Le Fanu. «I hardly know.»

The fire pops, sending up a skitter of sparks behind the screen. William sips his cocoa, a slight chill raising the hairs on the back of his neck. Walter drops a cool hand there and presses forefinger and thumb into the divots at the base of William's skull.

He sets aside the cocoa and eats the cake in four swift bites, then downs the brandy. The sugar settles his spinning head. The brandy makes it spin again, more pleasantly. Walter begins to massage the tense muscles beneath his scalp. He leans heavily into the touch and closes his eyes.

He doesn't want to break the idyll. He wants to forget about the war. This new revelation should be enough to crowd it out. But nothing can crowd out the death of the known world. Even Walter isn't impervious to that.

He speaks to arrest Walter's hand, which has slipped from the nape of his neck to the crook of his jaw, whose gentle touch threatens to distract him more thoroughly than the revelation of Walter's nature. «But I know now you could do what I asked.»

Walter's knuckles are still against his throat, and their proximity feels suddenly dangerous.

«Maria Moraru,» William says. He can feel his pulse against the back of Walter's hand. «You really could get her out of Bucharest.»

A moment of silence strung tight as catgut, as piercing as catgut bowed. Then:

«You are stubborn,» says Walter briskly, and takes away the tea tray.

«It would be *easy* for you,» insists William. «It's probably harder for you *not* to do it.»

«Harder for me to say no to you?»

«That isn't what I—»

«I have refused the wishes of much greater men, more times than you could possibly imagine.» The words are so cold they might as well be rimed with frost. But he is not looking at William; he is staring fiercely at the middle distance, jaw clenched. The way he had looked when he spoke about the lindens of Bucharest, and said he had not felt safe in his own city.

«Are you frightened to go back?» asks William. Yes, Walter has already done so several times, but of his own accord, to reclaim things that were precious to him—his paintings, mainly. The people under his protection.

Walter does not look up. His jaw does not relax.

«Was it really so bad as that?» asks William.

Walter draws long, dextrous fingers down the join between two strips of mink pelts, tracing the coverlet's seams. «It takes a human lifetime to accustom oneself to the idea of death,» he says. «And even longer to accustom oneself to its absence. I have found it difficult to reconcile my mind to the renewed possibility of my own demise.»

William can't help it—he laughs. Walter's eyes narrow, pained lines at their corners like fractures in a stone about to give way. But William has lived with death breathing down his neck so long that the idea of Walter struggling to reacquaint himself with mortality after almost five hundred years, the pain in his voice as he confesses it… what else can he do but laugh?

«I'm sorry,» he says, although he isn't. His chest hurts, but only from laughing, and that freedom makes him nasty, playful, careless with his words. He, who must always be so careful with them. Was this how Gerald felt when he was drunk? No wonder he drank so often. «Am I supposed to feel sorry for you?»

If Walter's sadness is unearthly still, his anger is the snap of sap boiling in a fire, the sudden explosion of sparks. Furious motion, albeit contained within the form of a man, rather than the fireplace's grate. Contained, but barely. Walter has made fists in the coverlet, his grip breaking the slippery guard hairs of the mink. William has put more space between himself and Walter without realizing it, and feels the cold air at the edge of the bed against his thigh. It is like the time a shell dropped on a church that he and Gerald had been admiring in some rural town in France. One moment he was running his palm along the big faces of the stone, the next he was twenty feet back with no memory of moving, no memory of the explosion. Only in retrospect did he realize he must have heard the whistling approach and run. Instinct, Gerald said. The same thing that tells the mouse to hide from the hawk, the deer to run from the wolf even before it sees him.

He remembers Walter snarling outside Mme. Popescu's house. The flash of the light on his bared teeth, the slam of the car door. But he remembers, too, the realization that followed: that the fuel of Walter's anger is his shame. His need to reach out is strangled by some self-defeating impulse to isolate himself. He, who must be so isolated already.

The fury passes; Walter doesn't pounce. William eases himself back toward the center of the bed. His blood is pounding in his throat, his ears, and he wonders if Walter can tell. His skin feels fragile, his body vulnerable in a new, exhilarating way.

With delicacy, with fear, he asks a question which has just occurred to him: «Are there any others like you?»

Walter loosens his grip on the coverlet. His palms sparkle with shards of glossy fur. «Not any longer. Not that I have met.»

Before he asks the next question, he thinks ruefully of Mihai: *you want to change his mind.* «Can you…make others?»

«Maybe,» Walter says. «But I have never tried.»

«Why not?»

Silence. Walter will not meet his eyes.

«Are you afraid?» he asks, and hears the echo. Afraid of death in Bucharest, afraid of whatever William is asking now.

Now Walter has moved away, to his side of the bed, without William's having noticed. His back is turned, and he is staring at the blackness of the window. «You have weeks left, maybe months,» he says at last, like it pains him. William is strangely flattered, until Walter goes on: «And you couldn't bear to spend them in the company of your wife. I must live with the consequences of my mistakes much longer.»

He's angry first. Livid. He opens his mouth to retort but realizes he has nothing to say. He is like Walter, anger boiling up from shame. Yes, Syrie was a great mistake, but he shouldn't be ashamed of his choice, which he made for the right reasons. It's other choices that haunt him. Better lives that could have been.

He licks his lips, looks down. Makes himself look up again. «Sometimes the mistake is letting go.»

Walter's voice is low and desperate. «Don't tempt me.»

«Tempt you?» William laughs again at the absurdity. He is dying, *now.* «Tempt *you?*»

Walter makes a frantic, wretched noise: a struck child, a stepped-on cat. He surges from the bed and sweeps the tea tray from the table. The cocoa pot spirals across the floor, splattering a nautilus pattern from its spout. Walter snatches his dressing gown from the Chinese screen and disappears out the door.

William sits alone in the firelight, heart pounding, adrenaline lighting up his veins. The smell of spilled cocoa makes him nauseous. He waits an hour, two, but Walter doesn't return. Eventually, exhausted, he falls asleep.

In the morning, the curtains are wide open. Winter sunlight pours in blinding sheets across the room. The other side of the bed is empty. Walter is nowhere to be seen.

William's evening clothes are freshly brushed and hung on the valet stand, his studs and cufflinks laid out in a ceramic tray. Shoes, freshly shined. Their soles send crisp echoes down the staircase. Florea meets him at the bottom with his coat and hat.

«Has M. Roşu gone out?» asks William. The manservant smiles tightly and does not answer. Outside, William has to shield his eyes with his hand against the glare of sun on snow. No, he thinks. Roşu has not gone out. Not in the light of day.

THEY ARE ENGAGED to visit a tiny gallery of antique pictures that evening, a place Walter assured him he would find exquisite examples of Orthodox religious art, even in these straightened times. People can't buy meat, the price of coffee has gone up even since he arrived, but here a wizened old man still sells icons and insists they're precious.

«This one,» says the proprietor, «I almost had to sell to a German lieutenant. He offered me nearly too much to refuse. But I would be happier to sell to you.»

It shows the harrowing of Hell. Jesus robed in white and gold, fallen gates beneath his feet recalling the crucifix. Death trampled down by death. The proprietor explains all this. William does not buy the icon—if the war has proved anything to him it is that death doesn't stop more death, but flows into it like snowmelt into a spring flood. And this Jesus, with his dark beard and mane of hair, nose thin and straight as a pencil, this Jesus reminds him too much of Walter, who has missed their appointment. Walter, who could trample William's death, but won't.

He does not write or ring or wire. A week goes by and William—pathetic, he hates that he does it, is he eighteen years old?—goes to Walter's house. Florea regretfully informs him that M. Roşu is not at home. William isn't even sure it's a polite fiction; no lights show behind the glass.

The fever comes back.

He has lost the plot of the story he wanted to write, the one about Sadie Thompson. He wishes he could write to Gerald to ask what he recalls of the missionary couple. Gerald who was *there*, who lived in the rainy boarding house and listened to the phonograph grind out the same records over and over and might remind him all these people's lives were real.

But one way or another, torpedoes, drink, or distance, Gerald is gone. And William let him go. Turnabout, he supposes, is fair play.

He *does* get letters from Syrie, arriving in a clump one afternoon with the diplomatic bag. They're fluff, fluff, pleas for money, what would he think if she repapered the dining room in white and gold? Silly stories about people whose names he doesn't recognize, as though she thinks he knows her friends, or cares. As though his life is part of hers. But even though he married her he's never been her companion. Not like that. The whole crumbling façade was built on her fear and his obligation and resentment.

Has he *ever* been anyone's companion like that? He might have hoped, with Gerald, but…but he was always *using* him. Gerald, so gregarious, sure of himself, younger and braver and apt to get into all kinds of conversations, situations, spots of trouble. Gerald always blazed the social trail and then guided William after, a naturalist collecting specimens for study.

What about Sue?

Well, what about her? No point in asking that question now, not when she's married the man and his title who got her in the family way. William tries to conjure up any bitterness at that: Sue snagging a much more eligible man the same way Syrie snagged him.

Except he can't imagine Sue would be any happier with her lordling. Which leads him to reflect, morosely, that Syrie can't possibly be happy with him either. If he wrote it as a play—two unhappy couples, both marriages built on the shaky foundation of paternal duty, star-crossed love between the wrong mother and father—there would be lots of laughs and a happy ending. Wouldn't Syrie enjoy being married to the Earl of Antrim's second son?

Things being how they are, writing it into a play is the closest he'll come to marrying Sue. And he hasn't the stomach for drawing room comedies anymore. The cynicism, yes, but none of the joy remains.

Maybe he should have knocked Sue up instead of Syrie. Oh well. Too late now. Too late now for much of anything at all, except regret. He wonders if Walter, undying, is capable of the same. Surely he must be, or he wouldn't fear connection as much as he does.

Walter doesn't write, but Max does, and William goes back to the chilly office with its vast windows in need of a wash. No more snow has fallen, and what remains is gray and greasy. It's the end of February, the long tail of Jassy's winter dragging sluggishly toward spring. He's been forty four a whole month now. He doesn't remember marking his birthday. He feels very old, but much too young to die.

"Any progress?" Max looks positively cheerful—the office is in boxes, which he is going over and cross-checking against a list. He is leaving, it transpires, at the beginning of March. And so is every other allied diplomat. William's mandate is now simply to exfiltrate Maria if possible, and come home before he can't leave at all, if the Bureau doesn't send for him first. Frankly, he expects the Bureau to recall him any minute. But as Max told him in the early days of his assignment, London is worlds away from the situation here.

"Of a sort," says William. Because in his loneliness, his tail-chasing and fevers and coughing and missing Gerald and Sue and yes, god damn it, Walter, he has concocted a very stupid plan.

Max looks surprised, and ceases cataloguing his files to sit still behind his desk. "Really? Roşu says he'll do it?"

William shrugs, which is not a lie. "There are some… requirements for the job."

"Naturally," says Max, unconcerned. Then, stepping back a pace to consider: "Amazing. No one else has been able to crack him."

That startles William. "You've had people try?"

"Of course," says Max. "He sounded useful. But I couldn't even get someone through his door, 'til now. Bravo. Can't imagine how you did it."

Perhaps the single benefit of Syrie's very public divorce for adultery, the scandal of Liza, their subsequent marriage: when every gossip rag in London makes it clear you've fucked a woman, nobody ever thinks you'd do the same thing with a man.

"These requirements," says Max. "What are they?"

"An ambulance," says William, "And money for emergencies."

Max blinks at him. "That's it?"

The skepticism makes him wish for a moment he'd been more extravagant. But then, Walter has never needed the Bureau's help before. William is wary of asking for too much lest he raise suspicions. "Yes sir."

Max shrugs and reaches for a pad of carbon paper requisition forms. He signs the blank top sheet, then slides the pad across the desk to William. "Fill that out and take it downstairs. They'll sort you out."

An ambulance and cash are not the sum of his requirements. Before he leaves Jassy he calls on Maria Popescu once more.

It is late, and raining: the kind of cold that is worse than snow. At first it feels good on his cheeks, which are hot. Eventually it has him shivering under his coat and muffler, drenched in sweat and freezing. His joints ache like an old man's, though he'll never get any older than this.

The low sky is purplish-orange, reflecting Jassy's urban glow. No blackout orders here, not now. Mme. Popescu's curtains are drawn against the chill, but warm light shows through the gaps. At first the maid does not want to let him in, but William is very practiced in waiting quietly through other people's protests, and it always seems to disarm them. The maid finally admits him to the parlor, then goes to hunt for the mistress of the house.

When she appears she looks hastily put together, hair precarious in its pins. «M. Maugham,» she says. «This is unexpected.»

«I'm very sorry to intrude.» He stands, holding his hat in his hands, the picture of humility. He wants more than anything to lie down. «It's important.»

She waves the maid away and gestures for William to follow her to the drawing room, where there is a fire in the grate and a novel laid face-down on the seat of a chair.

«Please,» she says, indicating the empty sofa. She does not offer him a drink. Instead, she remains standing for a moment after he has settled and then asks him, not altogether kindly, «To what do I owe this unexpected pleasure?»

Very fair. «I need a favor.»

She descends into her armchair, setting aside her novel. «Another one,» she says, picking delicately at a loose thread in the upholstery. «Of course. May I ask when you intend to *return* these favors?»

They both know the answer is never. He doesn't bother lying about it. «Your German friends—»

«They *aren't* my friends.» She is unexpectedly vehement. «I just think they may be useful.»

«Sooner than later,» he says.

She lays her head back, dark waves haloed by the antimacassar. Like the icons in the little shop. «What do you need, M. Maugham?»

«I need to get to Bucharest.»

She closes her eyes and laughs, firelight shadowing the lines in her face; she is a beautiful woman, but not a young one, and very, very tired.

«So,» she says, «Walter will not do a favor as easily as I will. Is that it?»

He had only asked for an introduction but Mme. Popescu is not an idiot, and she knows what Walter can do—*can you blame me for making a few demands?*. He wonders if she knows *all* that he can do.

William finds his left hand has drifted to the inside of his thigh, thumb just brushing the seam of his fly. He swallows and laces his fingers together in his lap. «Have you…heard from M. Roşu lately?»

Her laughter has not quite run out. «No more recently than you have.» Then she takes pity on him. «Gossip says he's sailed to South America, or at least tried. It's a gamble to cross the Atlantic these days.»

Well he knows. Walter is as much in South America as Gerald is at the front.

«Then again,» Mme. Popescu goes on, «I'm not sure Walter *can* drown.»

That answers that question. He wants to soften the next one with some meaningless pablum: *forgive my impertinence*, maybe, but the effort is too great and he suspects she would see through it. So he just says: «You were lovers.»

She cuts her gaze toward him low and sharp: the warning flick of a knife. «Does that bother you?»

It doesn't. And even if it did, Walter's gone. He shakes his head.

«That isn't why we fight.» She has not met William's eyes during this conversation, not once, but she does now. «My husband was an officer. I didn't want him to go to the front. Look around you; I'm wealthy enough he didn't have to. But.» She slaps the flat plane above her breasts hard enough he can hear the echo. «His sense of duty. And now I have no husband. So tell me, what kind of duty is that?»

Any sympathy he could offer would ring as hollow as her palm against her chest.

«He was gassed,» she goes on. «At Mărășești, last summer. They sent him home, but it had ruined his lungs.»

William thinks about taking deep breaths of morning air—the swell of his belly inside his waistcoat, the ache of the cold beneath his shoulder blades, behind his ribs. The rush of blood to his head. The freedom of it. The unbelievable ease. Now each of his breaths is a struggle, his lungs inflamed, the muscles of his back tight with shivering. He almost wishes he could stop. Almost.

«I watched him die every day, for a month,» she says. «But Walter…»

He doesn't want to finish for her; he knows too well how that feels. Knows too well how all of this feels.

«I loved my husband,» she says. «And I thought Walter loved me. Maybe I asked too much of that love. But now I think, perhaps I didn't ask the right way. Or that I shouldn't have asked at all. He is the kind of man who prefers to give a gift, rather than do a favor. And he was a prince, you know. He has that sense of noblesse oblige.»

The fever doesn't leave him now. It's never gone when he wakes up. He barely sleeps through nights, tossing and turning and half-dreaming. Sue, Gerald, the medical tents of France. Syrie's embrace slowly melting into the strangling grip of an octopus, a python, a horrible many-armed monster. The many-armed monster melting into French mud full of corpses, closing over his head. But never the dream of Walter again, because it wasn't a dream to begin with.

His final days in Jassy he spends largely on his own. He spent most of his childhood alone, and most of his young adulthood. His first bit of war work also alone, and never more so than on the deck of the steamer crossing Lake Geneva in the moonless dark of wintertime. Fitting he should be alone for the last bit of his war work too. Maybe the last bit of his anything.

The land is flat and lightless, the night without a moon and the sky thickly spangled with stars. The road is bad and the suspension on the ambulance is negligible. The ruts and the cold have conspired to numb his feet, his legs, his rear on the wooden bench seat, but every pothole sends a jolt up his spine into his skull. It keeps him awake, at least.

He is wearing a Romanian army uniform, too big for him in the chest and shoulders, stiff collar gapping around his throat. There is a tidy monogram stitched inside the lapel of the uniform's overcoat: MR. He wonders what the R is for; he never learned Mihai's surname.

Poor boy, who will wake up alone in William's flat with only William's clothes to wear—nothing that will fit him, if his uniform is any indication.

He wants to be pleased with his own daring; he wants to feel dashing and clever. Instead he feels exhausted, too cold and too hot all at once. From mile to mile it's hard to remember what he's doing, why he's here. Then a particularly deep rut will jostle some sense back into his head. Maria Moraru. Bucharest. Nobody else will. Not even Walter, who could do it easily.

So why should he? Why is he driving alone across this flat plain east of the Carpathians, half-delirious with fever, to rescue an agent whose intelligence probably isn't worth what the Bureau is spending to collect her? Why should he have done any of this? Any of the war work? Come to think of it, why even marry Syrie?

Maybe because he knows a thing or two about being left behind. And it's not something he'd wish on anybody.

A streak of white light shocks him out of his maudlin thoughts: carbide lanterns up ahead. The checkpoint outside of Focșani. This is why he stole the uniform. It is risky to be a Romanian soldier out on the road to Bucharest at night; to be English is a death sentence.

He lets the ambulance roll to a stop at the checkpoint, and keeps both hands on the wheel.

„Papers" says the hard-bitten Gefreiter, the plosive letting loose a rolling cloud of steam.

William takes a deep breath—or tries to. The cold air makes his chest seize, and then he's bent over the steering wheel seeing stars. By the time he looks up again the soldiers have had time to grow nervous, and their hands are tight on their Mausers. He's forced to admit the coughing fit did have very theatrical timing.

„Papers," the Gefreiter says again, this time an order. William reaches very slowly for the inner pocket of his coat, brushing Mihai's monogram with his knuckles. The muzzles of the Mausers rise another three inches, and jump up when he pulls his hand out. The white flag of his folded pass sends them slowly back toward the frozen ground.

The Gefreiter takes the packet from him and unfolds it, scanning the seal in the unforgiving carbide glare.

It's genuine—the passes aren't forged. Mme. Popescu's pet German officers have obliged their hostess in every particular. And Mme. Popescu has obliged William, perhaps out of pity. Or perhaps because she wants to show him that she's not like Walter.

„Your business in Bucharest?" asks the Gefreiter.

„Medical relief," says William, curt as he can, not sure what German spoken with a Romanian accent should sound like.

The Gefreiter laughs, and hands his papers back. „Poor fucker," he says, and at first William thinks he means, what rotten luck to land this job. But then he says „You learned German in the Rhine!"

Which is true enough. William grimaces and shrugs. „Heidelberg," he says. „At university."

The Gefreiter spits and laughs again. „Don't worry," he says, „We'll have all of you speaking good Bavarian German soon enough. Let him through!"

The rest of the squad sling their Mausers over their shoulders and jog to move the sawhorses and coils of barbed wire that block the road. William eases the ambulance past and is soon out of the patch of sharp white light and plunged back into darkness. The sounds of the soldiers laughing, mocking his Palatine accent, slowly fade into the distance. When the world has gone silent around him, he pulls over and cuts the engine. The shakes come like a rush of wind, starting at the top of his head and blowing through the rest of his body all the way to his toes, setting every nerve trembling like a leaf.

Occupied territory is just as quiet and dark as free, until he reaches the outskirts of Bucharest. This is where things go wrong.

Dawn is barely beginning to bleach the eastern sky, weakening the power of the floodlights. In the powdery blue gloaming the monotonous flat land and its sprinkling of ugly buildings feels two-dimensional and surreal. The German army camp straddles the road like a small stage set, peopled with actors in army costume.

Enter William, in an ambulance.

They go through the scene: Halt! Who are you? Papers, please. And hurry up! His head feels like it is floating three feet above his neck and slightly to the left. He feels like he is watching a tired Romanian soldier speaking his provincial German lines to the guards; the gray-faced man behind the steering wheel is a character in a little drama he has written.

The distance does not make him less invested; after all, isn't the power of drama that it commands the viewer's empathy? Even from the cheap seats, he cares desperately what happens to this little man on the stage. Please, please let him get through.

He watches himself hand the papers to the officer in charge, watches him perform the same inspection as the Gefreiter at Focșani. But something doesn't satisfy him, and he calls his second in command to take a look. They confer quietly, and then the officer draws his sidearm and uses it to wave William and his ambulance to the side of the road.

„Stay here," he says, and sets one man in front of the ambulance and one behind. Their guns touch his bumpers, little bites of steel on steel. The officer and his flunky retreat to the sentry box behind the barbed wire. William catches a glimpse of the flunky offering the bulky box of the field telephone, the officer holding the earpiece tight to his head, face pinched as he listens.

Well. It was always a terrible idea, always bound to fail. Just like it was supposed to. Poor Maria. Poor Syrie and Liza. And, how funny: Poor Walter. Half a millennium of being left behind, and William just the latest.

He rests his forehead on the steering wheel, fists numb and clenched on either side of his face. A raw wind skims across the fields and camp and snatches at exhaust smoke, whips up dust from the side of the road. It stings his face, sticks in his lungs. Wearily, William begins to cough. And cough. And cough.

He waits for the fit to stop, tries to hold his breath to calm the irritation in his lungs. But it doesn't stop and he can't hold his breath: his body betrays him, frantically sucking in great aching lungfuls of smoky, dusty, freezing air. His heart beat hammers in his ears.

He is still coughing when the officer returns.

„The proposal for this relief mission was denied," he says. He waves the papers at William. „Word was sent; you should not have come. You are not permitted to enter the city."

So much for Mme. Popescu's friends. Even if William had a rejoinder, an excuse, he cannot get the breath for it.

„Why did you come?" barks the officer. „What is your business in Bucharest?"

Tears are gathering in his lashes, snot trickling over his lips and mingling with his blood. There is more blood than he has seen before. Maybe too much.

He treated consumptives at St. Thomas's; he's read the literature on pulmonary hemorrhage, and seen it kill firsthand. A little spotting on the handkerchief is only dangerous because it can excite a patient. Their terror at the sight of it is more deleterious than the bleeding itself. Usually all that's required is bed rest, quiet, perhaps a calmative drug. But in Lambeth rest was a precious commodity, and though easily prescribed it could rarely be obtained. War, he has learned, is much the same as Lambeth.

„Corporal!" The officer is yelling at him from the end of a long tunnel. A fleck of spit hits his cheek. The Mausers at his bumpers are looking at him, bottomless black eyes.

So Mihai was a corporal. He fumbles at his lapel, finds the monogram with his thumb. Wonders if they'll shoot him before he bleeds out. It would probably be a more pleasant death. Quicker, at least.

He is still wondering when the officer stops shouting. In the sudden quiet he hears distant cries and agitation. Gravel crunches beneath the officer's heel as he turns away. He speaks, at first irritated, then with increasing agitation: „Sir? Sir! You cannot come through there. Sir—!"

The pop of gunfire makes William flinch, but he isn't hit. When the screaming starts, he realizes they aren't aiming at him.

Well, he thinks, as the black curtain of unconsciousness descends. What a melodramatic way to end the scene.

AT FIRST HE thinks he's fallen asleep while driving and dreamt the checkpoint disaster, because it's the potholes that wake him.

But he's lying down, not behind the wheel. He makes a noise of protest before he has time to think: he might be a prisoner, in which case it's better to keep still and quiet and listen.

Too late. A cool hand on his forehead. «Be still.»

A guarantee he'll do the opposite. He opens his eyes and tries to sit. "Walter? What—"

Walter holds his shoulder, one-handed and implacably strong. "*Still.*"

William subsides. He looks around. He is in a stretcher in the back of the ambulance. The canvas ripples and snaps in the wind, letting in flickers of gray daylight around the edges. Walter's hand remains on his shoulder. It is sheathed in blood. His cuff is soaked in it. It stains

Mihai's overcoat where Walter has touched, is touching. Red handprints on the blue-gray wool. He looks up and Walter's beard is dripping, his face a gory mask. His hair is damp, the ends of the curls sharply pointed like sable brushes wet with ink. Even his eyebrows are slicked down to his skin. William becomes aware of the smell.

He reaches for his own throat, clasping it like a choking man, but finds his own collar buttoned securely. His neck is dry and whole.

"It is not yours," says Walter.

Oh. The screams.

"Who's driving?» he asks. His voice sounds hoarse and strange. He realizes he's speaking English, and Walter is too.

"Maria," he says, and smiles. His teeth are white and startling under all the red.

When William wakes again, he is in a familiar bed, weighed down by the mink coverlet. Cool blue daylight comes through the window. Rain is tapping on the glass. The room is hot, and he can hear both the ticking of the radiators and the crackle and snap of the fire. A bead of sweat threads its way along his hairline and falls into his ear. He swallows. His throat is dry. The ever-present fever makes the sheets itch against his naked skin.

Someone shifts beside the bed–someone he can't see past the swell of blankets.

"Walter?" He tries to lift his head, expecting the press of a restraining hand.

Instead, a woman's face appears above his own. «You are awake!»

Her French is awkward and heavily accented. Her hair is loose, recently washed and only beginning to dry. Given another hour by the fire, he imagines it might be light brown, dark blonde. Her eyes are huge and luminous, pale green. Her narrow, sloping shoulders barely support the heavy brocade of a man's—Walter's?—dressing gown. She wears nothing underneath.

«You are thirsty?» she asks, and brandishes a glass of water at him.

"Maria?" he says. "Oh, good." And then he's slipping under again.

He wakes some time later and she's still there, hair fully dry and falling over her shoulder in a heavy braid. Someone—Florea?—has given her a striped flannel nightshirt to put on beneath the robe, but it gaps over one golden thigh. He can't see her knee, her calf, but he imagines an old scab, the sharp line of her shin bone, her toes curled into the thick pile of Walter's Persian rug like Sue used to curl her toes into the sheets. She is eating from a tray: a roll with butter, a dry cured sausage, a bottle of wine.

He wishes it were nineteen twelve. Nineteen ten. That this were England and he were a young man in good health, waking up to a beautiful woman in his room. Instead:

«Your report.» A great effort, and still barely audible. But she has clearly been listening for him to wake, and she lifts her head from her tea. «You need...» a pause for breath. «...To go to the embassy.» And then: «Gilbert Max. He wants your report.»

The cutlery chatters on the tray when she sets it aside. He feels the mattress dip, realizes his eyes have fallen closed. He forces them open again.

«Sorry,» she says, but doesn't look it. «I have no report.»

Even if that's what she thinks, it isn't true. A few days of debrief and she'll find out how much she knows. «You need to go,» he says.

Her frown is eloquent, dismissive. «My report is: Germans like to get their dicks wet, same as all of you.»

He is too tired to press her on this. Max didn't want her intelligence anyway. Max is done with this corner of the world. William is almost done with it too. His left ear is pressed to the pillow and he can hear his pulse there: tachycardia. If Walter put his teeth to any of William's arteries now, the blood would pop from him like champagne from a sabered bottle. Maybe that would be a relief.

«I think it is better if we all die,» she says, and William, half-hoping in vague terms for his own demise, thinks she is honestly proposing some kind of suicide pact.

It must show in his face—whatever he's feeling. Maybe surprise? She laughs and leans forward, brushing his sweat-soaked hair back from his forehead. Like Sue, in his dreams, but not like Sue. Her hand isn't soft—the last several years haven't been easy for anyone. He still lets his face fall into her palm.

«I will go to Paris,» she says. «Walter says he can take me.»

That's when he realizes she means fake their own deaths. Disappear.

He could go missing. Assumed dead. Do what he came to Romania to do, without having to do it. Except he will, in the end. Just not on the cold road between Jassy and Bucharest, alone except for German soldiers.

They all will, in the end. Except for Walter.

«Did M. Roşu say…when he came for you. What did he say?»

«He say, "You leave now if you want to leave at all."»

«But why?» He tries to lift his head, sit straighter, but Maria makes a face and pushes him brusquely down. He goes. He's too weak not to.

«You need rest,» she says, and starts to stand.

He wants to wrench an arm out from beneath the mink and grab her wrist. He can't. «Did he say *why?*»

She pauses, bites her lip, then shakes her head. «No. Only: the English get my message.» She settles again on the edge of the bed and considers him. Her frank appraisal makes him embarrassed of his naked weakness, the sweat in his hair.

«Will you go back?» she asks. «To the English?»

He isn't going anywhere. He may not even leave this bed. «What will you do…in Paris?»

She looks down at her hands, curled in the folds of Walter's brocade dressing gown. «My children,» she says. «They are there. I send them when the war starts, to be with my cousin. Her husband has one leg, can't fight. He fixes shoes.» Her smile shows she's well aware of the irony. «Better there, for them, I think. And I'm right.»

He likes her answer much better than any he would have come up with. «Tell me about them,» he says, and drifts off listening.

AND THEN IT'S night. Deep night, and the fire burning very low. A scratchy piano lullaby is playing on the phonograph: Fauré's Berceuse from the Dolly suite. The jewel box insularity of the room and the divorced feeling of the fever give everything the quality of a dream. But a dream onto which the concerns of the waking world intrude. He's monstrously thirsty, his tongue like blotting paper.

"I'll—" he starts, then tries again, marshaling his French. «I'll take that water now.»

The sound of silk on upholstery. Footsteps cushioned by the thick pile of carpet. And then Walter, his face clean and white as Roman statuary, beard neatly trimmed and brushed. When William cannot hold the glass he takes a paper straw from the bedside table and drops it into the water, then tips the glass and straw so William can drink. When he's done, Walter takes the glass away but holds it in readiness.

«Did you kill the whole section?» William asks. He doesn't have much breath to put behind the words. They come out mostly consonants.

«And the men at Focșani.»

No more Gefreiter with his good Bavarian German. «God, what a mess. Max…will be livid.» He sighs under the mink. The pelts are heavy as another body on top of his own. A hundred small dead weights. «He thinks it's you.»

Walter's eyebrows lift.

«Rescuing Maria.»

«Well in the end, I did.»

He should say thank you but instead he says, «Why?»

A long pause. The record ends and the phonograph begins to hiss. Walter rises to remove it, and William lets the answer to his question slide through his fingers; his grip on life has grown loose and he hasn't the will to tighten it.

Walter lifts the needle.

«I like the modern composers,» he says, into the hush. «Ravel, Satie, Fauré, Debussy. I think they make the piano speak, as Bach did for the cello.»

William laughs, weak and overwhelmed. «And you remember when Bach was new.»

«Sometimes.» The click of the cabinet—he has put the record away. «Other times, it doesn't seem worth the effort.»

«Remembering?»

«I've made a lot of memories.» Walter sits back down on the bed. «It takes some digging, and I don't always like what I find.»

«Do you regret it?» William asks. «What you are?»

The divot comes into Walter's brow again. William is past fear. He reaches out and puts his fingers over Walter's, but is too weak to grasp his hand. «I won't laugh this time. I promise.»

Walter smooths one hand across the mink coverlet, and the guard hairs lie straight and flat behind it. He does not look up at William, but he turns his palm up and takes William's hand in his. His grip is careful, and there is a tremor in it: he wants to hold more strongly. He is afraid to. When he speaks, his words are just as careful.

«I regret,» he says, «some of the choices I have made.»

M. Popescu—what rank did he die with?—coughing up his ruined lungs. Mme. Popescu embittered. Five hundred years worth of other broken hearts and missed opportunities. Five hundred years of leaving people behind. Of being left.

If William had known that Sue would leave him, and so would Gerald, would he have left them first? Would abandoning Syrie and Liza have hurt him more or less than doing right by them? Would he have saved himself any pain, or would the pain have found him no matter what? Does it truly cost less to be alone, or is the cost only in a different currency? Funny little bank notes in a matchbox. Lei and Deutchmarks in tidy bundles, hidden under the driver's seat. Foreign money never feels as real.

He should give that money to Maria, for her children.

«Why *did* you rescue her?» he asks. Why break half a century's streak?

Walter's thumb presses his knuckles. «I wanted to do something for you. But I was afraid to give you what I most wanted to give. And you did want Maria, so.»

And now he has her. She's safe and whole, in vibrant living color just like he imagined she would be. Duty discharged. But oh, he doesn't feel like he is done. Maybe one's duty is never discharged. Maybe there is no such thing as duty: only a twitch upon the thousand threads that keep one bound to life.

William lifts Walter's hand—a Herculean effort—and lays its cold weight in the center of his chest, above his laboring heart. «Are you still afraid?»

Walter leans close. His lips brush William's throat when he says, «Yes.»

∞

ACKNOWLEDGEMENTS

This book would not exist without Novella Club, to whom it is dedicated: Jackie Kay, Julia Sterling, Rachel Sobel, and Rebekah White. Nor would it exist without my persistent editor and publisher, dave ring, who kept asking me when I would write a novella for him, no matter how many times I insisted I didn't know how.

Jay Wolf, as always, and Huw Evans. I don't think I can write a book without either and/or both of you at this point.

Dr. Sorin Cristescu and Dr. Geoffrey Swain for their wealth of historical and political knowledge about WWI-era Russia and Romania. All errors, elisions, and artistic license are my own.

Saika and CD Covington for German dialect assistance, and Eric Roberts for military history consultation. Now that Twitter is a thing of the past I don't know how I'm going to get excellent help like theirs at short notice.

Thank you finally to the Alpha Workshop for Young Writers class of 2023, and staffers and guest authors—being surrounded by your enthusiasm and creative intelligence helped me survive several difficult revisions of this manuscript.

ABOUT THE AUTHOR

Lara Elena Donnelly is the author of *Base Notes* and the Amberlough Dossier, and a co-founder of the small press Homeward Books. She lives in Harlem with a fashionable film buff and a talking cat.

ABOUT THE PRESS

Neon Hemlock is a Washington, DC-based small press publishing speculative fiction, rad zines, and queer chapbooks. Publishers Weekly once called us "the apex of queer speculative fiction publishing" and we're still beaming. Learn more about us at neonhemlock.com and on social medias at @neonhemlock.